He'd saved her again. Now *she* needed to save *him*...

One of the gunmen was taking careful aim.

Trina put the pedal to the metal. The Tacoma lurched, and the would-be shooter shrieked and leaped aside. Never slow on the uptake, Rogan leaped out and onto the ground and then sprang into the pickup.

"Let's go," he cried, rolling down his window. He stuck his pistol outside and sent a pair of shots back toward their assailants.

"We'll have to follow the route that's already plowed, which will head us toward town. We can't go deeper into the mountains."

"Do it," he said. "These guys won't be able to follow us any time soon. Just get us out of that sniper's range."

As if to mock Rogan's words, glass shattered behind her, and pain blossomed white-hot through Trina's left shoulder.

She lost her grip on the steering wheel and the Tacoma slewed toward a snowbank.

Maybe they weren't going to make it out alive after all...

Jill Elizabeth Nelson writes what she likes to read—faith-based tales of adventure seasoned with romance. Parts of the year find her and her husband on the international mission field. Other parts find them at home in rural Minnesota, surrounded by the woods and prairie and four grown children and young grandchildren. More about Jill and her books can be found at jillelizabethnelson.com or Facebook.com/jillelizabethnelson.author.

Books by Jill Elizabeth Nelson

Love Inspired Suspense

Evidence of Murder
Witness to Murder
Calculated Revenge
Legacy of Lies
Betrayal on the Border
Frame-Up
Shake Down
Rocky Mountain Sabotage
Duty to Defend
Lone Survivor
The Baby's Defender
Hunted for Christmas

Visit the Author Profile page at Harlequin.com.

Hunted for Christmas

Jill Elizabeth Nelson

If you purchased this book without a cover you should be aware that this book is stolen property. It was reported as "unsold and destroyed" to the publisher, and neither the author nor the publisher has received any payment for this "stripped book."

PLEASE RECYCLE • THIS PRODUCT IS RECYCLABLE •

Recycling programs for this product may not exist in your area.

ISBN-13: 978-1-335-40316-2

Hunted for Christmas

Copyright © 2020 by Jill Elizabeth Nelson

All rights reserved. No part of this book may be used or reproduced in any manner whatsoever without written permission except in the case of brief quotations embodied in critical articles and reviews.

This is a work of fiction. Names, characters, places and incidents are either the product of the author's imagination or are used fictitiously. Any resemblance to actual persons, living or dead, businesses, companies, events or locales is entirely coincidental.

This edition published by arrangement with Harlequin Books S.A.

For questions and comments about the quality of this book, please contact us at CustomerService@Harlequin.com.

Love Inspired
22 Adelaide St. West, 40th Floor
Toronto, Ontario M5H 4E3, Canada
www.Harlequin.com

Printed in U.S.A.

From the end of the earth will I cry unto thee,
when my heart is overwhelmed: lead me to the rock
that is higher than I.

—*Psalm* 61:2

To the brave and dedicated men and women
on the front lines of the war against drugs.

ONE

Trina Lopez released a pent-up breath as she guided her four-wheel drive pickup into the driveway of her rural home nestled in the Wind River mountain range of Wyoming. Tension unwound from her muscles. *Home at last. Thank You, Lord.* The blizzard that had scoured her vehicle with whistling winds and buckets of snow since halfway between her friends' ranch and her own had turned the twenty-minute journey into more than twice that much.

This morning, when she'd left to attend the birth of a new foal, the meteorologist on the radio had been predicting another ten-inch dump of snow, starting sometime in the afternoon. A sensible person would have stayed home, but as the only veterinarian within a hundred miles, Trina didn't have that luxury. People and their animals depended on her. It was a life she loved.

Then why did her heart sit heavy like a shriveled lump of coal in her chest?

Firming her jaw, Trina peered ahead as the pickup rolled effortlessly through inches of new powder.

With dusk closing in and curtains of white billowing in the keening wind, the long, low ranch house with its attached veterinary clinic and surgery was only a dark blob. To the left of the house, the machine shed formed a slightly more compact blob, and to the right, her barn loomed, a tall and sturdy shadow. She headed the pickup toward the barn and finally glided under the shelter of the lean-to attached to the building.

Trina shut off the ignition and slumped to rest her forehead on the steering wheel. The *tick-tick-tick* of the cooling engine echoed the beat of her pulse. It was times like these, when the weather and the darkness closed in, that she most keenly missed the people who used to be the center of her life.

A plaintive moo sounded from the interior of the barn, and Trina lifted her head with a grimace. "I'm coming, Sunshine."

Clearly, her cow was all too aware that supper was overdue. Zipping up her down-filled jacket, Trina stepped out into the bitter cold. On the short trek to the barn, wind-driven snowflakes lashed her face. She opened the barn door and stepped inside. At least the temperature was much warmer out of the wind, but the memories pummeled her instead.

Her Shoshone father, the leather-tough former marine William Longrider, had succumbed to a sudden brain aneurysm this spring. Trina had found him here in their barn, chores half-done, but well gone from this world. At first she'd walked numbly through each day, and then she'd allowed the usual heavy summer workload to keep her occupied from dawn until well after dark. But fall had brought a lonely Thanksgiving, and now… *Merry Christmas to me.* She'd yet to muster any enthusiasm for her favorite holiday, and the calendar said the celebration of Christ's birth lay less than two weeks away. With her marine husband, Richard Lopez, buried eight years ago as a casualty of an IED in Afghanistan, and now her father gone, she was discovering firsthand the truth of the saying that holidays were the worst for the bereaved.

Squaring her shoulders, she flipped the light switch, and several overhead bulbs diffused dim illumination over the large space. Her horse, Luca, stuck his dappled-gray head over his stall door and whickered. Trina headed for the stacks of hay bales piled to one side of the door. Luca neighed, and a sudden bang announced a hoof hitting the wooden side of his stall.

Trina halted. What was making her horse nervous? She could understand the cow wanting her supper, but Luca never kicked. And where were the cats? Normally they swarmed her ankles when she appeared. They only hid when a stranger was present. The hairs on the nape of Trina's neck prickled. Her ears strained to catch the slightest whisper of foreign sound.

There! A tiny rustle in the loose hay in the corner behind the bales. Most likely a wild critter had found a way to sneak inside out of the foul weather. Trina snatched up a pitchfork from a wall rack and the heavy-duty flashlight kept on the shelf beside it. Flashlight beam leading the way into the gloom-shrouded corner, she crept toward where she'd heard the noise.

A dark figure lay propped in a sitting position

against the wall with long, jeans-clad legs stretched out straight. Human, yes, but since the person was bundled in a bulky coat and the face was shrouded in shadow, she couldn't tell the gender. A motorcycle helmet and gloves lay near the person's side. What idiot would brave the mountains on a motorcycle this time of year, especially when a storm was brewing?

Pitchfork at the ready, Trina drew closer and trained her light on the person's face. A man, judging by several days' growth of dark beard on a bold jaw beneath an aquiline nose. The skin above the facial hair was tanned and smooth, and the thick-lashed eyes were closed. Unconscious?

Suddenly, the eyes popped open. Bluer than she'd ever seen in a sunny sky, but colder than frost. She gasped and pulled back.

The man's arm raised, and a pistol barrel stared her in the face. Trina swallowed against a dry throat. Her gaze followed the man's arm down to the part of his left side that had been covered by it. A telltale shade of red she well knew in her occupation soaked the side of the man's jacket.

"Don't move a muscle," the wounded stranger growled. "Are you a sicario sent after me by Trent Stathem or the rat from the DEA?"

A chill wound its way around her spine. A sicario? An enforcer for a drug cartel? Why would this man think such a thing about her?

"I have no idea what you're talking about," she said. "Who are you, and what are you doing in my barn?"

"*Your* barn?"

"Yes."

"You live here." The pistol lowered marginally.

"Most of my life." Trina's grip tightened around the handle of the pitchfork. Useless item against a gun. She'd best keep this guy talking and hope for an opening to disarm him. "What's this about cartel enforcers and DEA rats? Are you hiding from the law?"

"I *am* the law. Undercover DEA agent."

"Seriously?"

Should she believe him or not? The weapon slowly lowering until it came to rest against his thigh tended to bolster his case. A crook would have kept his gun pointed at her—unless he was too weak from his injury to hold the weight up any longer. His pallor and the amount of red on his jacket suggested significant blood loss.

"I'm sorry," the man said, his words slurring slightly, as if he were battling to hang on to consciousness. "I don't mean to bother you, and I don't want to involve you in my mess. If I'd had any other option, I wouldn't be here, but the storm forced me to find shelter. Once it passes, I'll be on my way. That is, if you can spare me some gas for my Harley. It's parked behind the barn."

Trina let out a soft snort worthy of Luca. "Ride out of here on a motorcycle in your condition? I don't think—"

A crash and an inpouring of frigid air announced the barn door flying open. Trina whirled to find a second gunman leaping into the building, pistol brandished. The man rushed toward her, teeth bared above the scarf that ringed his neck and chin.

"Where is the traitor?" the man snarled, aiming the gun at her. "Tell me quick, or I'll put one in you now."

Trina's heart stalled. Her mouth fell open, but no words filled it.

"I'm here," called the wounded stranger.

From the corner of her eye, Trina detected movement as the injured man struggled to his feet, pistol rising. Cursing, the newly arrived gunman shoved Trina out of his way. She staggered backward against a stack of bales, which tumbled sideways, and she fell flat among them. Loose hay flew around her, tickling her face and filling her nostrils with a musty, grassy scent.

The men fired at nearly the same instant—one shot a swift echo of the other. Her animals reacted with their own native noises, creating a din of moos and whinnies. Blinking rapidly and swiping hay out of her face, Trina regained her feet to find the second intruder laid out motionless on the floor. Instinctively, she grabbed the gun from his flaccid hand and turned toward her first uninvited guest. The man who had claimed to be a federal agent stood propped against the barn wall, his weapon extended toward the gunman on the floor.

"Drop the gun," she bit out.

"My pleasure," he muttered, and his pistol hit the floor with a soft *thunk*.

The man's eyes rolled back in his head, and his knees slowly buckled. He slid to the ground, leaving a trail of blood on the wood behind him.

Fresh awareness crept up on Rogan McNally in stealthy degrees. He was warm and lying on something soft and comfortable, though an ache pierced his left side just below his rib cage. His eyelids weighed too much to lift, but his ears were picking up faint sounds—a muted crackle and someone's soft footfalls nearby. His nose appeared to be working as it was capturing smells. Antiseptic with a metallic backdrop. Blood. Yeah, he'd lost more than a little. And another odor. Pleasant. Burning wood. Must be the source of the crackle.

Gathering every ounce of strength, Rogan lifted his eyelids far enough to squint at his surroundings. The white ceiling of a room swam into view. Was he in a hospital? He didn't know any hospitals with fireplaces in the patient rooms. He swiveled his eyes to the left. Log cabin wall. He swept his eyes to the right. An interior wall painted pale blue, a wooden door in the middle of it. He looked down. Sheet and blanket covered him from chin to toes.

Just beyond the carved wood footboard of the bed in which he lay, and directly in front of the fireplace on the far wall, stood a tall, lean woman—the one who had found him in the barn. Her rich mahogany eyes gazed solemnly at him. He judged her to be in her early thirties, about his own age. She was dressed in blue jeans and a green plaid button-up shirt. Long, straight hair, sleek and black as a raven's wing, was pulled back severely from her face in a ponytail, emphasizing her widow's peak above the thick arch of dark eyebrows. The face was completed by a pair of high cheekbones, a narrow arrow of a nose, a generous mouth drawn into a frown and a strong, square chin. A classic beauty she was not, but she had something more timeless—an arresting quality of dignity and strength.

"Where am I?" His voice whispered between bone-dry lips.

"My guest bedroom." The woman's mouth thinned. "Though I did consider just trussing you up and leaving you in the barn with the body of that other gunslinger until the sheriff collects you."

Rogan couldn't fault her for remaining suspicious of him, especially since he'd held a gun on her. Under similar circumstances, *he'd* be suspicious of him, too. But for her sake as well as his own, he needed to get out of here before the sheriff showed up.

"The other guy didn't make it?" he asked.

"You're a good shot. I'll give you that." Her tone belied any compliment in the words.

Rogan's heart pinched. In that moment, it had been kill or be killed, but that didn't make taking a life any easier.

"Thank you for helping me," he rasped, "but who are you?"

"The person who loaded your sorry carcass onto a sled and hauled you into my surgery to treat your bullet wound."

"You're a doctor?"

"Veterinarian." The full mouth curved slightly upward at the edges as amusement lit the dark gaze. "I had to use small animal sutures and calculate equine antibiotic to an appropriate dosage for a human roughly six feet tall and about a hundred and eighty pounds.

Now, I think it is time for you to explain who *you* are." Her eyes narrowed at him. "A DEA agent? Really?"

Reflexively, his tongue darted out to moisten his lips. What should he tell her? His cover name, Ryan Osborne? Or should he introduce himself by his real name? Didn't matter much. Three long years of undercover work had been blown along with his identity. Might as well take the opportunity to be himself.

"My name's Rogan. Rogan McNally."

"I'll have to take your word for it, because your pockets contained no wallet, no ID of any sort. Only a *lot* of cash." She waved a hand toward the bedside table.

He glanced in that direction to find his folded and rubber-banded wad of hundred-dollar bills perched there like a stack of accusation. A pang struck him as if he'd done something wrong, but he hadn't. Yet the circumstantial evidence must make him seem more crook than cop to her.

"I asked you before, and I'm going to ask you again. I want the truth. Are you a fugitive from the law, Mr. McNally?" She folded her arms across her chest.

Rogan met her dark gaze. "No…and yes."

"Being cryptic doesn't serve you well when you are at my mercy after threatening me with a gun."

An involuntary chuckle escaped his chest, sparking pain in his side. "Sorry about that." He groaned. "I assumed you were one of those who want me dead. But if that were true, I already would be."

"Who wants you dead? This Stathem you mentioned or the Drug Enforcement Administration?"

"Anyone from Trent Stathem's drug-running crew

that I had infiltrated or the mole in the agency. As I told you, I'm an undercover DEA agent. I was betrayed by someone in my own organization. Now I'm—"

"On the run," she finished for him.

"I was going to say being hunted. Once I'm on my feet again, I plan to turn the tables and do some hunting of my own."

"Ambitious." The woman smiled, displaying straight, white teeth, but her gaze remained cool and assessing. "Why should I believe you? A badge is another thing I didn't find when I was treating you."

"Undercovers don't carry badges."

"Fair enough. Where did you come from on that motorcycle?"

"Rock Springs."

Her brows raised at the mention of the small southern Wyoming city. "You drove a hundred miles?"

"Sometimes you grit your teeth and go or you die. Had to shoot my way out of a bad corner and didn't get away without a souvenir." He touched the bandage wrapped around his lower chest. "How long have I been here?" He couldn't afford much time laid up in bed, as badly as he needed it.

"Less than twenty-four hours. The rest did you good, but you need more. Let me get a little soup into you first." She started toward the door.

"Wait!"

The woman stopped and gazed over her shoulder at him.

"I don't even know your name."

"You can call me Dr. Lopez."

He struggled to sit up on one elbow.

"Take it easy, Mr. McNally." She turned and stretched her hands toward him, palms out.

"I can't, Dr. Lopez. You mentioned the sheriff coming." A tingle shot up his spine. "The wrong person aware of my location could seal my death warrant… and yours, too, for getting involved with me."

He packed as much sincerity into his gaze as he could muster. She needed to believe him, as much for her own sake as his. The people he was dealing with wouldn't leave witnesses.

A frown furrowed her brow. "Noted, but I trust Sheriff Bosworth."

His gut clenched. "How soon will he be here?"

"Relax." The doctor huffed. "The blizzard let up less than an hour ago, and night is closing in. It will be sometime tomorrow or maybe even the next day before anyone can get to us this deep in the mountains. In the meantime, I'm going to feed you some soup then let you sleep again. Don't worry. I'll be nearby, double-barreled shotgun within reach, every minute."

Rogan settled back onto the pillow with a grudging smile on his lips. Canny woman. She was letting him know that she was prepared for anything—either more of his enemies showing up with mayhem on their minds or himself turning out to be a lying weasel about being law enforcement and trying to get the drop on her again. Not that he was capable of the latter right now. The last time he'd felt this weak he was eleven years old and recovering from double pneumonia.

His hands fisted. Helplessness stunk. Especially

when an innocent Good Samaritan could pay the ultimate price because he didn't have the strength to haul himself out of bed. His enemies would have been monitoring the law enforcement chatter throughout the state. If Dr. Lopez had contacted that sheriff she trusted so much, whether the sheriff was dirty or not, the wrong people would know his location. More killers would be coming for him soon—and anyone who had helped him.

"You need to believe me," he said as her hand closed around the doorknob. "If they can find a way to get here before the sheriff, they'll make it happen. You can count on it, Doc. They're coming."

TWO

You can count on it, Doc. They're coming.

Bathed in the cozy light and warmth of the blaze in her living room fireplace, Trina sat in her rocking easy chair. Rogan McNally's words played like a looped recording through her head. She'd made sure her unwelcome guest ate some soup, and then she'd left him to sleep more. Best thing for him.

Trina glanced toward the guest room door. Pity she couldn't lock it from the outside. He might seem as sincere as the day was long, but she had no proof that he was law enforcement like he claimed. For all she knew, he could be a desperate criminal. But she couldn't afford to ignore his words about more people being after him. People like the guy who had attacked them in the barn—the kind who would take *her* out, too, without a second thought. After the fierce blizzard, the stone silence outside seemed weighted. Or perhaps the word was *waiting*, as if holding its breath for the next sort of storm to break.

Trina's gaze drifted up to the fireplace mantel,

where she'd set out the manger scene that her father had hand carved. He'd whittled away on it, sitting by the fire, during the very year when she came back to Wyoming to stay after her husband was killed and she left the military base on the East Coast where she'd spent her married life. Dad had been so pleased when she married a marine like he'd been, and he'd known exactly how to comfort her when she lost her husband. Part of that comfort was the traditions they kept together, like the way they decorated at Christmas—an aromatic, fresh tree from their backyard, garland on the mantelpiece and brightly colored lights wound around the porch railing. Now, the nativity set was the only nod toward the Christmas season she'd been able to muster.

Lord, I'm so glad You were born, but even You had family around you in that stable. I have no one.

An acrid tang coated her mouth. Was that what she was turning into—a bitter, lonely woman? She had to snap out of it. After all, she had a home, a fulfilling career, good friends and her animals. She should be thankful. She *would* be thankful.

She reached down and stroked the soft fur of her collie, Chica, lying beside her chair. The animal heaved a contented sigh but didn't lift her head from her paws. Chica was young and inexperienced, not savvy like old Brown, her previous collie, but Brown was gone now, and Trina was training this one to be a good ranch dog. However, what Chica lacked in experience she made up for in acute hearing, a quality that Brown had nearly lost before his passing. The young collie would alert her well before human ears could detect the approach of outsiders. It would be up to Trina to determine if the intruder was innocent wildlife passing by outside or two-legged varmints with evil intentions.

"Keep your ears open," she told the dog as she rose from her chair.

Chica lifted her head from her paws and blinked acknowledgment then settled down once more. Smiling, Trina stretched her arms, shoulders and spine then hefted her shotgun that had been leaning against her chair. She might as well grab some sort of rest. Cradling the gun in the crook of one arm, she passed the coffee table, where she'd laid out most of her additional arsenal of weapons, a collection not atypical of any mountain rancher, then stretched out on the sofa and allowed her eyes to drift closed.

She had no idea how much later it was when a guttural growl roused her from fitful slumber. She sat up with a start. Chica stood facing the front of the house with her ears pricked and the ruff of her neck standing on end. Trina heard nothing—yet.

"Good dog," she said as she stepped toward the front window, feet guided by the waning glow of the logs in her fireplace.

Stopping just outside the curtains, she turned her head and listened. There it was—faint but unmistakable—the buzz of snowmobile engines. The small hairs on the back of her arms prickled. Even as she stood there, the noise grew louder, closer. Locals out for a joyride in the wee hours? Not likely.

She turned toward Chica. "Are we ready to defend our home?"

The collie responded with a throaty woof.

Grimacing, Trina headed for the guest room. Whether she fully trusted McNally or not, she needed to alert him. She opened the door to find him sitting up in bed.

"They're coming." He turned a steady gaze toward her.

"You have sharp ears," she said.

"Would you at least bring me my shirt?" His face and torso were in shadow, but the bandage around his middle stood out stark white in the dimness. "I'd rather not greet these guys in nothing but my jeans."

"I had to toss your bloody shirt in the garbage. I still have some of my dad's clothes. I'll dig out an old T-shirt of his. It'll probably be too short on you, but it should fit around the shoulders. He was a beefy guy. Ex-marine."

"Did he teach you how to shoot?" McNally jerked his chin toward the shotgun in her hands.

Trina's heart panged, missing her father afresh. "He taught me a lot of useful things."

She brought him the shirt, and soon the alleged DEA agent emerged into the living room fully clad. Somehow, despite his wound, he'd even managed to pull on his socks and the steel-toed work boots she'd removed from his feet before tucking his unconscious form into bed. The man's tousled brown hair was a bit long for her taste, but he seemed to have a strong face beneath that unshaven scruff. And despite his injury, his blue gaze was alert and steady. The man clearly kept himself in good shape. If he were any less fit, he might not have survived the blood loss from his gunshot wound. Nor would he have managed to make it this deep into the mountains in this weather on a motorcycle.

Tough guy. Both her dad and her husband would have admired his grit. The jury was still out for Trina regarding this man's character, though she couldn't help acknowledging his rugged appeal. Good thing she'd promised herself after Rick's death never again to let herself be attracted to any guy in a dangerous occupation.

"I don't suppose you want to trust me with a firearm." He sent her a lopsided grin, gazing toward the arsenal of handguns and ammunition, as well as a pair of rifles and his own pistol laid out on her coffee table.

"Let's wait and see what our visitors do. Maybe they just want to talk." At least he gained trust points for not diving after a gun without permission.

He snorted. "This will be Stathem's goons, and they won't waste any time on preliminaries. By the sound of it, they're almost here."

The grating buzz saw of the engines had grown quite loud.

Trina shook her head. "In the bowl of this valley, sounds are amplified. I'm used to it. They're probably a good half mile away yet. When the wind's not howling, there's no sneaking up on this place."

"How did the guy I shot sneak up on us?"

She rolled a shoulder in a shrug. "The wind *was* howling, and he left his sedan at the side of the road on top of the ridge. Hoofed it in. I found the car and left it where it was. Don't want to mess up any forensic evidence."

Her guest exhaled a long, heavy breath. "For what it's worth, I'm truly sorry you're caught up in my mess."

"What did you want me to do? Toss you into a snowbank and forget about you? Even if you were a known serial killer, I would still have treated your injury."

"I appreciate that, and I am who I say I am." His blue gaze darkened. "Let's survive this, okay?"

"I make out the sounds of at least three different engines. Probably three guys minimum, six max, right?"

He nodded. "That's a fair guess."

"What kind of firepower will they be coming with?"

"Top of the line. Automatics for sure. Possibly flashbangs to disorient us or even full-on grenades. And they'll probably post a sniper somewhere in case they flush us out and we try to run."

Trina's pulse accelerated, her heart beating a tattoo against her ribs. *Steady on*, she told herself. She'd assumed most of that already from what she'd heard or read in the news about how modern drug cartels operated. The information was pertinent for all residents in the area, because the drug trade flourished everywhere around them—the small towns, the larger ones and the nearby Wind River Reservation—with meth labs hidden in the mountains and other drugs funneling into and out of Wyoming on the interstate highways.

"Good thing I took your first warning seriously," she told the enigma standing in her living room. "I prepared a few surprises outside for unwelcome guests." She could only pray that she'd done enough.

"Let's get ready in here, then."

Together they tipped Trina's heavy dining room table on its side as a makeshift shield. Then she grabbed Chica's collar, ushered her into the laundry room and closed the door. The collie wasn't an attack dog and would only get in the way or get herself killed in a skirmish. She arrived back in the main room to find that McNally had moved the coffee table with its firepower to a location behind the dining table, and he was checking the loads in her guns. At her appearance he put down the revolver he held and lifted his hands in a surrender gesture.

Trina halted, gaze locked with his. She had a decision to make. Did she believe he was a DEA agent as he claimed to be or not? Either way, if those people out there were out to kill this wounded man in her home, as well as anyone with him, then they had a common enemy.

One by one, the engines outside shut off and silence descended once more. No voice called toward the house, friendly or otherwise. A bad sign of bad intentions. She was going to have to trust McNally and hope she wasn't making a mistake.

She nodded toward the man. "Take your pick, but we don't start anything unless they do, and we don't shoot to kill if we can help it. I'm wired to save life, not take it."

"Agreed." He scooped up his pistol.

There was no more time to second-guess herself.

A pane of her mullioned front window shattered, and a heavy object flew into her living room on a gust of frigid air. The object blew up, spewing noxious smoke. A firm hand grabbed Trina's arm and dragged her, coughing and choking, down behind the cover of the table. A pained, masculine howl sounded from her porch. Crouched beside her, McNally's questioning gaze snagged hers.

"Bear trap under the window," she rasped out.

"One down," he rasped back.

Trina's front door burst inward, followed by a spate of automatic fire. McNally dropped sideways, peered around the table's edge and returned fire. Another male howl. Trina scooted to the other side of the table, took aim and let loose one barrel of her shotgun at the lower extremities of a second guy charging through the open door. He went down and joined his comrade rolling on the floor and clutching his knee.

A great crash came from the back entrance. Trina's hair stood on end. From there, two doors led to this part of the house. One choice would take the assailant through the mudroom, the other through the laundry room, where her collie was stashed. The dog suddenly let out a piercing yelp.

Chica!

Without a second thought, Trina charged for the back of the house, ratcheting the load into the second barrel of her gun. Behind her, McNally hollered for her to stop, but she paid no heed. Wrecking her house and shooting at *her* was one thing but messing with her animals was quite another.

As she rushed through the laundry room door, a hand snaked out and wrenched the shotgun from her grip. It went off but peppered only the ceiling. Trina was jerked up against a hard chest, and a gun barrel dug into her temple on one side while the hot breath of her captor puffed into her ear on the other side. Chica cowered in the corner beyond the dryer, whimpering. Had the gunman kicked her? A growl left Trina's throat.

"Be still now," said a deep voice in her ear. Then the man's head lifted away from her. "Come out, come out, wherever you are, Ryan or Rogan or whatever your *real* name is," the man called. "Show yourself or the woman gets it right now."

No response, except for rustles and pained curses from the wounded men in the living room. Her captor called out again with more threats. Then one of the snowmobiles' engines revved to life. Trina's gut shriveled. Why had she ever trusted a man who had held her at gunpoint the first moment they met? McNally had abandoned her, and now she was going to die.

Gripping the doc's Tikka T3X hunting rifle and scarcely daring to breathe, Rogan took up a position to one the side of the laundry room door. Hot wetness was spreading again on his side, and pain vied for his attention. He ignored it. No time for weakness. Especially not when he was about to go up against Manny Fenton, one of the most ruthless enforcers on Stathem's crew. Hearing that familiar, cold voice had nearly frozen the blood in his veins.

With a cry, the doc stumbled through the doorway,

no doubt shoved by Fenton. The man himself followed on her heels with his gun pointed at her back. Fenton's attention was aimed toward the front yard, where the snowmobile engine purred. Quick as a striking snake, Rogan slammed the enforcer's arm down with the barrel of the rifle then whipped the butt around and rammed it into the guy's head. Fenton slumped to the floor.

The doc whirled in a self-defense posture. Her gaze widened on him, and fight ebbed from her stance.

He offered her a slight smile. "Meet Manny Fenton, stone-cold killer." He motioned toward the man on the floor.

She glanced at the fallen figure then looked up and blinked at him. "You didn't leave? But I thought..." Her words trailed away on a stare toward the sound of the snowmobile.

Rogan pulled a set of keys from his jeans pocket and jingled them. "Took these from one of those dudes on the floor. It has a—"

"Remote start," she finished for him. "Let's get these guys tied up and ready for the sheriff."

"On it," he said, motioning to the pair on the floor.

In obtaining the snowmobile keys, he'd also hurriedly secured their hands with the belts of their snowsuits. Their legs were already incapacitated, though no longer bleeding profusely. Now they lay there moaning and calling him bad names. He hadn't known the man he shot in the barn—possibly a freelancer out for any reward on him that Stathem would have broadcast throughout the underworld. But he knew this pair—

Mickey Groves and Nathan Snyder—almost as much bad news as Fenton. Stathem had sent his best after Rogan, and they'd been taken down by a wounded man and a civilian veterinarian. It would make quite a story if he ever had the chance to tell it.

"Think you can handle the guy in the bear trap on the porch?" the doc asked. "I need to see to my dog before I do what I can for our attackers."

Her voice trembled a bit. Fading adrenaline, no doubt. Her raw courage was beyond dispute.

Rogan nodded. "I'm going to exercise a little caution, though. The guy on the porch could still take a shot at me when I poke my head out, and we might yet have a sniper on the ridge."

A faint shriek suddenly echoed from the ridgeline.

The doc smirked. "Someone I loved taught me what to look for in a good sniper nest. While you were sleeping this afternoon, I located a couple likely spots up there and set snares. I must have picked rightly. I imagine our would-be sniper is now hanging upside down from a tree by one leg."

Rogan chuckled, winced at a stab of pain from his side and composed himself. She got an A-plus for ingenuity, too.

"Your marine father was a trained sniper?"

"No, my marine husband, Rick, before he was killed in Afghanistan."

Her expression shuttered, and she turned away to head into the laundry room. A soft canine whine greeted her appearance, and the doc responded in soothing murmurs.

Rogan soon had the man on the porch subdued and bound. Turned out to be some lowlife Rogan hadn't met before, but the guy had tried to take a potshot from where he sat tethered to the porch boards by the large-toothed trap around his ankle. Looking into the barrel of the doc's fine rifle had discouraged resistance. It took every bit of Rogan's waning strength to free the gunman from the bear trap and drag him into the dubious shelter of the living room, where he lay grousing and complaining beside his comrades.

The hole in the front window was letting in significant amounts of cold air even though he'd managed to close the damaged front door. Rogan started shivering and pressed his hand to the wetness on his side. His palm came away red.

Dr. Lopez showed up, trailed by a collie dog. The animal crouched down near their captives, growled low in its throat and bared its teeth. The trio on the floor paled and fell silent.

The doc chuckled. "Chica has a little aggression in her after all."

"Good for her. Now, what about our upside-down sniper?"

"It'll be daybreak soon. When visibility is good, I'll go up and collect him."

"I should be the one to do that."

"Not hardly." Her gaze dropped toward the blood-soaked T-shirt she'd lent him. "I'll stitch you up again, see to these guys' wounds and then you can guard them while I snowshoe up the ridge with a rope and a sled for binding and transporting our sniper."

Rogan opened his mouth to protest about the danger then closed it again. She could handle the assignment. Of that, he had no doubt. About himself, on the other hand, the weakness creeping through his limbs was not a good thing.

"You can call me Trina, by the way," she said as she restitched his wound while he sat on the couch with a blanket around his shoulders.

Warmth bloomed inside him that a mere blanket could not give. She finally trusted him. From the cool and cautious demeanor this woman had displayed, he could only assume her trust to be a great honor. What kind of history did this intriguing woman have in order to forge such competence and courage? A pair of military men in her life, for starters. Too bad he couldn't stick around to find out more. He'd brought enough danger into her life.

"Pleased to meet you, Trina," he said. "Call me Rogan. It may sound like a cliché, but when you call me Mr. McNally, I feel like you must be speaking to my father."

"Rest now, Rogan." She patted his shoulder and went to see to their wannabe killers.

They all behaved themselves as she delivered first aid. Partly because Rogan kept the rifle trained on them and partly because of the collie's steady, baleful stare. A short time later, she had tacked a hunk of plywood over the broken windowpane and was donning her winter wear.

As she headed for the door, her reloaded shotgun in hand, the dog rose as if to follow her.

"Stay," she said, and the animal subsided onto its haunches with a whine. "Obey Rogan." She said the words toward the dog but pointed at Rogan. The collie swiveled its head toward the sofa where he sat. "Rogan, this is Chica."

"Hi, Chica." He nodded toward the dog.

A few grumbly noises in the collie's throat indicated what Chica thought about her new orders, but she stayed put as Trina opened the door.

"Mind the kiddies." She winked at Rogan over her shoulder and was gone.

Rogan chuckled, appreciating the battlefield humor, then looked down at the painkillers in his hand that Trina had given him. He shook his head and pocketed the pills. They might make him drowsy. He had to prepare for what needed to be done. Gritting his teeth, he levered himself off the couch and onto his feet.

Chica lifted her head and gazed at him.

"Stay," he told her and headed into the guest room.

He needed to go off-grid fast and find a place to heal that wouldn't endanger anyone else. If he accessed the internet, he'd need to do it from a public server. If he used a phone, he'd need a burner. And if accommodations were required, however transiently, he'd have to pay for them in cash. He scooped the wad of bills from the bedside table and peeled off a few hundreds to pay for the repairs to Trina's house, any medical supplies she'd used and the rifle and ammo he was going to take. Then he stuffed the rest of the money into his jeans pocket. Yes, it was drug money he'd snatched from Stathem's operation when he had to run, but if—

no, when—he got this mess straightened out, he'd report every dime.

As soon as he was strong enough to handle any fallout that might occur, he had to make his move to discover who in his agency had betrayed him to the cartel. Courageous and compassionate Trina had no part in any of that. She'd done enough—more than enough. He needed to disappear from her life. With him gone, and these goons turned in to the law, there would be no reason for Stathem's crew to pay her any further attention.

He hoped.

Steeling himself against pain and physical weakness, he stripped the snowmobile suit from the gunman who had tried to use Trina as leverage against him. Fenton was the nearest thug to Rogan's size and was still unconscious, so he didn't object to being manhandled. Rogan checked all the captives' bindings again, and to make doubly sure they couldn't escape, he found clothesline in the laundry room and bound all of their ankles together, one to another. He earned a few extra curses for his antics, but he ignored the empty words.

As Rogan tied the last knot, a deep rumbling noise trickled faintly to his ears. Chica heard it as well and rose from her haunches with a bark. Rogan darted to the door and peered outside.

The sun had fully risen, its rays turning the fresh powder into glitter, but there was no sign of a motorized vehicle on the road beyond the snow-blanketed yard. He glanced toward the ridgeline that encircled the ranch. No sign of Trina, either. Too soon to expect her back. The rumbling grew louder, but the doc had said the bowl of the valley amplified sound. Whatever vehicle was approaching might not be as close as it sounded.

A snowplow? The engine did rumble like a diesel. With a plow would come law enforcement. Should he stay where he was and put himself in the hands of the sheriff Trina trusted? The idea was tempting, and the prospect of a long, morphine-enabled snooze in a hospital bed actually held some appeal. But, no, he'd be a sitting duck under care in a medical facility.

Particularly when he'd likely be handcuffed to the bed until his identity was verified through a call to his handler or the elite few at DEA headquarters in Virginia, who had originally sent him to Wyoming. Someone among that handful of people who knew his undercover identity had exposed him to the cartel just as he was about to complete his mission of identifying the shadowy kingpin who operated Trent Stathem's puppet strings. No, he needed to stick around long enough to make sure this sheriff of hers was trustworthy and would look after her, and then he needed to vanish.

"Sorry, Trina," he muttered as he gathered up weapons and ammunition.

"Stay," he told the dog again as he exited the front door into the crisp winter air.

God, I'm doing the right thing, aren't I?

His prayers had grown few and far between in the past few years in the very dark world he'd inhabited undercover, but he wanted to be sure about his actions, because leaving Trina behind carried some risk for her. Just not as much risk as keeping her with him. Though he suspected the latter would be against her will. She had a life here. No, he *was* doing the right thing. The only thing he could do and hope to stay alive and eventually get justice, not only for himself but for all the lives Stathem's drugs had destroyed.

Then why was his gut twisted into a Gordian knot as he loped toward the barn, where he would wait and watch until he was sure that the arrival of the sheriff brought safety to Trina as she expected?

The inside of the barn was significantly warmer than the outdoor air and laden with rich and not entirely unpleasant animal smells. A whicker from the horse greeted him, and straw rustled in the stalls.

Rogan located the ladder to the hayloft and climbed awkwardly, favoring his left side, to the vantage point height gave him. As he poked his head into the loft space, a bevy of cats scampered into shelter behind hay bales. Rogan ignored them as he hunkered down behind the shuttered opening intended to receive the bales at haying time. Rifle in hand, he unlatched the pair of shutters and nudged them open far enough to give him a clear view of the yard.

He'd been right about the approach of a snowplow. The enormous vehicle was just stopping in the yard with a large SUV coming to a halt behind it. The sheriff's office logo on the side of the SUV's door jumped out at him. If the sheriff had been alone in the vehicle or maybe with a deputy in the passenger seat, he'd have assessed the situation as normal. But he made out figures in the back seat as well. Not normal.

Movement coming into the yard drew his attention. Trina tromped toward the house pulling a small sled with a body trussed up on it like a Christmas goose. A grin formed on Rogan's face. The woman sure did her marine daddy and husband proud.

Trina lifted her hand in a wave toward the sheriff's vehicle, her shotgun held at ease by her side. A series of *pop-clicks* announced the SUV doors bursting open. Five armed men poured out, followed by two more from the cab of the snowplow. In moments, Trina was surrounded and disarmed.

A deep groan ripped from Rogan's throat. How was a lone wounded man supposed to pull off a rescue from a posse of thugs armed to the teeth? He had no idea. He just knew he had to do it.

Die trying was more like it.

THREE

Surrounded and weaponless, Trina looked from one hard-eyed face to another in the ring of thugs that surrounded her. Where was Rogan? Where was the sheriff, for that matter, since these thugs had arrived in his SUV? And what had happened to Jeff, the regular snowplow driver? Had this appalling chain of events resulted in casualties among her friends? Her gut twisted.

A short, stocky man stepped to the fore, invaded her personal space and put his doughy face within inches of hers. The man's black eyes glittered like slick onyx, and his hot and sour breath, steaming in the cold, turned her stomach.

"Where is he?" Each word clipped out like a standalone sentence.

Trina's throat went dry. She cleared it. "I've been asked that question before. And I never seem to know the answer."

The man's thick lips stretched into the semblance of a smile. "You are a cool and calm one."

Cool? He must not realize that her heart was trying valiantly to pound right out of her chest.

"Either that," he continued, taking a step away from her, "or you're too foolish to recognize the danger you're in. We're not people you want to mess with."

"I can see that, but your people attacked me without provocation in my home, and I've been defending it as best I can."

The man's expression froze, and then he burst out laughing. He waved his arm toward the sniper, cursing and red-faced, being released from his bonds by his fellow thugs.

"A most capable defense, I can see," the man continued. "Which proves my theory that you are some kind of law enforcement or perhaps ex–law enforcement friend of our quarry."

"I'm a veterinarian. The only occupation I've ever had. Ask your men inside. I'm an animal doctor, but I was able to adapt my skills to treat their wounds."

"After you inflicted them."

"There's that, I guess." Trina shrugged.

The man pursed his lips. "Very well, then, Doctor. Tell me where the traitor has gone, and you can return to your practice."

She truly *would* be a fool not to see the lie in this man's eyes. Somehow, she needed to keep the guy talking, stall for time, in case outside help was on the way or on the minuscule possibility Rogan could pull something off like he'd done with Fenton. What that might be, she couldn't imagine.

"First, tell me what you've done with the sheriff and the regular snowplow driver."

"So, you can give them aid?" Her captor's gaze took on a sly glint.

"If possible."

The man waved a dismissive hand. "Don't worry about them. They're taking a nap in the garage in Pinedale, where the snowplow is kept. Eventually someone will find and free them."

"You didn't kill them?"

"We only want to kill the traitor. Where is he?"

"Look," Trina said as she spread her empty hands, "this stranger arrived at my place uninvited while I wasn't home and took shelter in my barn. I—"

In a blur, the man's hand darted out and struck her cheek. The loud smack echoed in her head as she staggered from the stunning force. Cheek stinging like a hundred bees had attacked, she barely managed to keep her balance.

The guy was in her face again, gripping her scarf so tightly she gasped for air. "Do not even attempt to pretend you don't know Ryan Osborne. He came to you because he trusted you. Now, tell us where he is."

The man released his hold on her scarf. Trina gulped in a deep breath and rubbed her cheek and neck. Other than that, she held herself very still so her internal quaking would not show on the outside.

"I don't know a Ryan Osborne," she croaked out. "He introduced himself by another name."

Her tormenter's eyes narrowed. "Ah, then I was right. You must have known him from *before* he slithered into our ranks like a snake in our midst. And now your DEA friend Rogan McNally sought you out for aid. I will ask you one more time only. Answer or die. Where is he?"

"He ran off, boss," interrupted a voice from the porch.

Trina turned toward the broken doorway of her home, where the injured attackers were being helped outside. The gunman who had briefly held her captive glared at her with particular venom where he stood shivering, stripped of his snowsuit.

Had Rogan taken the suit? Did that mean he was long gone? If Rogan had left, did he think he was leading the danger away from her? Possibly. She didn't know him well, but he hadn't abandoned her like she'd thought when Fenton had put a gun to her head. She didn't want to jump to the wrong conclusion again. Maybe Rogan had heard the plow's diesel engine approaching and figured help was on its way for her and skedaddled. Whatever his reasoning, he was gone, and she was here, dealing with another invasion.

And where was Chica? The collie hadn't barked or made a sound when the men she was guarding were released. Rogan wouldn't have taken the dog with him, would he? Trina bit her lip against the impulse to call her collie. She didn't need Chica in the line of fire also.

With a face a shade of red that would have made a tomato proud, the boss man stalked toward the wounded thugs on the porch. "None of you thought to mention this earlier?"

Fenton's complexion went waxy, and his comrades,

supporting each other due to their wounded legs, tottered a few steps backward.

"Pah!" The man spat on the ground. "I'll deal with you later." Muttering curses that included words like *stupid* and *incompetent*, he returned to stand before Trina. "It's time to reward you for assisting the traitor. I'm sorry, but we can't have you helping him if he decides to double back this way."

"Let me do it, boss," Fenton offered.

His eagerness curdled Trina's stomach.

The boss snorted. "You're shivering so badly you couldn't hit the broad side of the doctor's barn. Go wait in the house until I decide what to do with those of you who failed me."

The sniper she'd trapped on the ridge stepped into the ring of thugs. "Let it be my privilege." A gloating smile stretching his lips, the man's dead eyes riveted on her.

"Be my guest." The boss issued a histrionic bow and backed away from Trina.

Her insides went as cold as the weather. *This is it, God? This is how my life ends?* She lifted her chin. No one would see Master Sergeant William Longrider's daughter and widow of Gunnery Sergeant Richard Lopez grovel.

The sniper began lifting his sidearm but halted, jaw dropping, as the snowplow engine roared to life. Every thug yelped and whirled toward the monster machine. The plow turned toward the gunmen then rumbled straight for them. Bullets began flying and people began running.

Trina seized the opportunity to tackle the thug who held her shotgun. The pair of them thudded to the ground, and fresh snow geysered into her face. Spluttering, she wrested the weapon from the startled man. As he drew back his fist to strike her, she jammed a thumb into his eye. He howled and covered his face with his hands as she rolled away and came to her feet, armed.

The plow was turning this way and that, keeping the thugs in front of it. The blade was raised to protect whoever was in the cab from the storm of bullets pinging off the thick metal. From the noise, if Trina didn't know she was in the midst of a firefight, she'd think someone was playing an out-of-control electronic pinball game, like the vintage model enshrined at the café in Pinedale.

No one appeared to be paying her any attention. Their bad.

In a crouching hustle, she slogged through the snow to the rear entrance of the house. Shouts and shrieks and gunfire continued from the front yard. A new sound—the crunch and groan of imploding metal—joined the bedlam. Whoever was in the cab of that plow must be taking out the SUV and snowmobiles. The action dovetailed perfectly with her getaway plan. She needed to move fast, because it would only be a matter of minutes before someone would get a clear shot at the plow driver.

It had to be Rogan. For some unidentifiable reason, the thought thrilled her heart.

Trina reached her kitchen, and Chica appeared, tail

wagging and tongue lolling, to greet her. The dog must have gone into hiding elsewhere in the house when more thugs started pouring through the front door.

"Smart girl," she told the collie.

Trina grabbed up the keys to her truck, her small handbag and her household first aid kit. No time to go to the surgery and get her more complete kit. She did take a moment to snag a pistol from her collection and tuck it into the rear waistband of her jeans. Then, waving for the dog to follow, she headed out the back door of her house.

The race to the barn, Chica at her side, took a small eternity through the fresh snow. Her quick glances at the bedlam in the yard confirmed that the drug dealer's crew was wising up and starting to flank the plow, but it also confirmed that the sheriff's SUV and the remaining snowmobiles were piles of wrecked metal.

At last Trina reached the barn lean-to where she had parked her truck. She wrenched open the driver's door, motioned Chica inside and followed the animal onto the seat. At a turn of the key, the engine purred to life. Without caution or hesitation, she rocketed out of the lean-to and whipped the steering wheel around to do a half doughnut, so she was facing the conflict.

A familiar dark head showed in the cab of the plow. Rogan, indeed. The guy was a bucketload of surprises. Her heart did a little skip. He'd saved her again when he could have run and saved himself. Now *she* needed to save *him*. One of the gunmen was standing clear of the fray and taking careful aim.

Trina put the pedal to the metal. The Tacoma

lurched, wheels spinning in the fresh powder, then grabbed traction and sprang forward. The would-be shooter must have caught sight of the movement from the corner of his eye, because he shrieked and leaped aside even as Trina guided the pickup to a near miss of his scrambling form. She performed another half doughnut, putting her truck's passenger door within feet of the plow's door. Never slow on the uptake, Rogan leaped out and onto the ground, her rifle in hand, and then sprang into the pickup.

"Let's go," he cried, rolling down his window. He stuck the rifle out and sent a pair of shots back toward their assailants.

Trina accelerated the Tacoma toward the road. "We'll have to follow the route that's already plowed, which will head us toward town. We can't go deeper into the mountains. Even this bad boy truck won't make it very far through an unplowed stretch of road."

"Do it," he said. "These guys won't be able to follow us any time soon. No vehicle. And I took the snowplow keys. Just get us out of that sniper's range."

As if to mock Rogan's words, glass shattered behind her, and pain blossomed white-hot through Trina's left shoulder. Her right hand flew reflexively to the wound, and she lost her grip on the steering wheel. The Tacoma slewed toward a snowbank. Maybe they weren't going to make it out alive after all.

"Trina!" Rogan cried as blood soaked her shoulder.

The pickup veered off course, heading them toward a snowbank on the opposite side of the road. Reaching around the dog, who let out a yip, he grabbed the wheel and turned them back on course.

"Hang in there," he said. "Let's get a little farther away from danger, then we can switch drivers."

"Not necessary." Her words emerged strained, as if through gritted teeth. "You're hurt, too. I can do this." Her right hand took control of the wheel.

"Debatable, but we need to stop soon, anyway, so I can bind up the wound."

"To that I can agree."

At the top of the ridge, they passed what Rogan made out as the corner of a vehicle sticking out of a snowbank. Must be the car Trina had said their assailant in the barn had driven. If their pursuers trotted up the ridge far enough to find the vehicle, he wished them lots of fun digging it out.

Under his watchful eye, Rogan allowed her to steer the truck another mile up the road.

"Stop now," he said. "We need to stanch the bleeding. We can see to further treatment when we put more distance between us and them."

Wordlessly, Trina stopped the truck but let the engine run. Thankfully, warm air was beginning to stream from the vents, somewhat counteracting the cold air wafting into the cab from the spiderwebbed hole in the rear window. Rogan shooed the collie into the rear seat of the club cab. Then, as gently as possible, he assisted her in removing her jacket. She had to be in major pain, but she gave no evidence other than a series of sharp intakes of breath. His respect for her went up another few notches.

"Looks like the bullet is embedded in the fleshy part of your upper arm," Rogan told her. "The brachial artery is on the underside of the arm, so it wasn't touched. We can be glad about that. You're bleeding, but you're not going to bleed out any time soon." He wrapped her knitted scarf around the area and pulled it tight, eliciting another sharp intake of breath.

"A wound like that hurts like nobody's business," he said, "but it should heal well if we get that bullet out soon and treat the site for infection. Just don't go into shock on me."

Trina let out a soft snicker. "I thought *I* was the medical expert. But I noticed in treating the wound on your side that you have a scar on your arm and another down your left rib cage—the kind of wound a knife might make. Been in a few fights?"

Rogan's throat tightened. "Comes with the territory."

The words emerged gruffer than he'd intended, as memories assailed him. He'd paid too dear a price in blood, sweat and tears to allow a filthy mole in the DEA to stop him from exposing the kingpin behind Stathem. Rogan was 85 percent sure who it was, but he'd held off from reporting his suspicions to his handler until he had the final proof. He'd need that proof to be believed. Now, he couldn't even think about making that report until he knew whom he could trust in his own agency.

"Undercover work?" she said.

"You have no idea what's required, and you don't *want* to know, believe me."

Those striking mahogany eyes pinned him beneath an assessing stare. A single, graceful brow arched high. "I've heard my fair share of war stories."

He offered a lopsided smile. "I'm sure you have, and you and I have just survived a personal war."

She shook her head. "A battle, yes, but the war's not over yet."

He had no argument to contradict her impeccable logic. "I think I should drive now. My injury won't affect my ability to handle the wheel."

At her frowning nod, Rogan got out of the truck and came around to the driver's side, while she scooted over. As if sensing her mistress's pain, the collie crept into the front seat and perched close to Trina with a soft whine. Rogan put the truck in gear and headed up the road. Only a single track slightly wider than the Tacoma was plowed. Snowbanks hugged them on both sides. Avoiding someone coming their direction would be a problem.

"Who was that short, stocky guy that seemed to be in charge?" Trina asked.

"Congratulations, you met Trent Stathem face-to-face." Rogan let out a humorless chuckle.

"The drug lord whose crew you infiltrated?"

"Drug underlord would be more accurate. I'm tasked with finding out who the boss's boss is."

"How was that mission coming?"

Several responses vied for supremacy on his lips, but the fewer specifics she knew the better for her.

"Tricky," he said at last.

She snorted. "Evasive, but I understand. The men

in my life shared stories, but there was a lot that my father did in the marines, and even more that my husband did, that they could never tell me." She turned her head away. "Stathem said they stashed the sheriff and the snowplow driver in the equipment garage before making off with their vehicles. He implied they're still alive."

"I don't know." Rogan shook his head. "Never take anything Stathem says at face value. He's slimier than pond scum."

Her heart drooped. "I was afraid you were going to say something like that."

"On the other hand, he can speak the truth just when you think everything coming out of his mouth has to be a lie."

"So, there's hope?"

"Always." He slid his hand along the seat, brushing past the dog's paws, and laid it over hers.

She sent him a look that he could only interpret as grateful. His heart expanded. A woman like this could get under his skin in a hurry, but now might rank as the worst moment in history—well, at least his own personal history—to entertain the slightest romantic interest.

Trina turned her head, eyes scanning their surroundings, which, from his perspective, were pretty much pine woods on steep, snow-covered slopes as far as the eye could see. But she seemed to see more than that, judging by the pursed lips and the nod.

"In about twenty to thirty minutes," she said, "we'll

come to my friends' ranch, Jim and Amy Miller. You can leave Chica and me there."

Rogan shook his head. "Chica, maybe, but not you. You haven't merely defeated Stathem's gunmen in a fight they brought to you. You've humiliated *him* personally. He won't forgive or forget that. Even if he took me out, he'd still come after you, and he won't hesitate to hurt anyone you're with."

"Awesome!" Trina's tone exuded irony. "So, we're on the run together until this guy is put away?"

"Thanks. I appreciate the vote of confidence." He flashed a grin then sobered. "I have a friend in the marshals' service that I trust absolutely. If we can get someplace where I can safely contact him, he could put you in protective custody."

She sent him a sharp stare. "Why don't you go into protection, too?"

"I've got a job to finish, and I need to be on the loose, not hiding under wraps, to do it."

The time passed all too slowly, but finally Trina indicated a driveway flanked by tall wooden signs advertising the Wind River Stables, offering trail rides and riding and roping lessons. Rogan guided the pickup into the driveway. None too soon—judging by the growing pallor and pinched lips on his passenger's face—they pulled up next to a low-slung ranch house similar in design to Trina's home, but without the attached veterinary clinic. Rogan helped her out of the pickup then half carried her up the steps onto the porch. Chica followed, whining softly. Evidently, the dog shared Rogan's concern about her mistress.

The door opened at his first knock. A full-figured, middle-aged woman gasped as her gaze settled on Trina slumped against him.

"What happened?" She flung the door wide. "Come in! Come in!"

They entered a warm and cheery kitchen decorated in country cute, featuring lots of chickens, roosters and sunflowers. A round-bellied man of medium height rose quickly from the table and strode toward them, abandoning a plate of eggs and a steaming cup of coffee. He helped Rogan guide Trina to a chair that their hostess pulled away from the kitchen table. Trina slumped down with a soft cry.

"You must be Jim and Amy. I'm DEA Agent Rogan McNally. Trina's been shot by drug smugglers who are after us."

At the bluntness of his statement, Amy gasped, and her dark eyes went wide.

Jim drew himself up stiff. "We've heard those people have been operating in the area. What do you need?"

"First, we have to get the bullet out of her upper arm."

"I'll call for an ambulance," the woman said, heading toward the landline phone on the wall.

"No!" Rogan's rough bark halted her, and she turned toward him, gaze sparking. "Sorry," he went on, "I didn't mean to sound harsh, but the people after us will be checking the hospitals. Nor is it safe for you to let anyone know that we've stopped here. The quicker we can leave, the better for you."

"I'm sorry, Amy, Jim." Trina's tone lacked its usual vigor. "I didn't know where else to go, who to trust."

"You've come to the right place," Jim affirmed with a nod.

"Would one of you be able to rcmove the bullet?" Rogan asked.

Amy's chin came up. "I'll do my best. On a ranch, I deal with many injuries."

"My first aid kit is in the truck," Trina said.

"No need. I have my own." The woman bustled to retrieve it from a cupboard.

Rogan went to the kitchen window, parted the curtains and peered out. Their enemies shouldn't be close on their trail, but he'd rather err on the side of caution. Stathem would already have made a phone call, summoning more of his people to provide transportation. The fresh rides could be passing by this ranch on the way to Trina's at any time. He needed to move the Tacoma out of sight.

Rogan turned toward his host. "Do you have any place I can hide Trina's truck?"

Jim's eyes glinted quick comprehension. "The drug dealers will know it?"

"I don't want to take that chance." When Stathem called for transportation, he would have been sure to include a description of the Tacoma and instructions to keep an eye out for it.

"Then I can do more than simply provide a temporary hiding place," Jim said. "I can offer alternate transportation."

"Show me."

Jim grabbed a heavy jacket from a hook on the wall and donned it while leading the way out the door. Rogan glanced over his shoulder to find Amy bent over Trina. The veterinarian's eyes were squeezed shut, and the muscles in her jaw pulsed as the rancher's wife dug for the bullet. Finger-shaped bruises were forming on Trina's cheek where Stathem had struck her. A slow burn began in Rogan's belly. Injuries due to violence were an understood risk in his profession, but a brave civilian should not be beaten and shot for showing kindness to a wounded man. Swallowing the growl that rose in his throat, Rogan left the house.

"Bring the truck and follow me to the machine shed," Jim told him.

Rogan drove the Tacoma across a yard that had been cleared of snow, no doubt by the skid loader that sat outside the machine shed. Jim opened the shed's double doors and guided him to a spot behind a tractor.

Rogan climbed out of the pickup, and the rancher waved him deeper into the cavernous space lit by bars of suspended fluorescent lights. Together, they strode up to a long, large, lumpy object covered by a canvas tarp. Jim whipped the tarp away and stood grinning like a fox in the henhouse.

"Everyone will look at you, but no one will see you in this," Jim said.

Rogan gaped. What in the world was a rural mountain rancher doing with a gleaming white limousine sporting dark-tinted windows?

FOUR

Standing in front of the dresser mirror in Jim and Amy's cozy bedroom, Trina gingerly slid the clean blouse Amy had lent her up over her injured shoulder. The bullet had been removed and the torn flesh disinfected and sutured. Now, a padded bandage covered the wound, yet her whole shoulder burned and ached. Holding her arm close to her body, she awkwardly did up the buttons on the blouse. The sound of a door opening and closing, followed by a burst of masculine voices, informed her that Rogan and Jim had come back to the house.

Trina hauled in a shaky breath and grimaced at the reflection of her pale, pinched face in the mirror. Time to return to the kitchen and discuss what needed to happen next. Going into some version of witness protection with the marshals' service held zero appeal. Her veterinary skills were needed here, and she had animals to look after at her ranch. Going on the run couldn't be the only option, could it? Maybe if they went to town and found the sheriff, Rogan could leave her in his care.

Surely, law enforcement from around the state would swoop in after an attack like today and send the bad guys into hiding. She'd be safe enough.

For a while.

Maybe.

Trina's stomach knotted. Was this Stathem really so vindictive he'd come after her—either now or later—no matter what? That's what Rogan seemed to think, and Rogan knew the guy—Trina didn't. All she had to go on was the darkness in the man's gaze that had nothing to do with the color of his eyes. She shivered, and a pang shot through her shoulder, a sharp reminder of how dangerous these people were. How ready to kill. Maybe she *didn't* have a choice. Perhaps fleeing was the only option. For now. Was she ready to trust her life to a wounded and hunted undercover agent?

Slowly, Trina's spine straightened, and her chin firmed. Despite their rocky introduction in her barn, Rogan had saved her life twice so far when he could simply have gotten away clean on his own. Once when that gunman Fenton had her and then again when he pulled that stunt with the snowplow. The shadow of a smile flickered on her lips. If the situation hadn't been so terrifying, she might have been amused by the looks on those thugs' faces while they dodged the plow blade.

"How are you doing?" Rogan's soft-voiced question drew her attention. His tall, sturdy figure, still dressed in the heavy snowsuit, stood framed in the doorway. His blue gaze was gentle yet assessing.

"The consensus seems to be that I'll live. And I could ask you the same question."

"Same. Aren't we a pair?" He offered a half grin. "Ready to go? Jim's come up with some novel transportation for us that nobody, but nobody, will think to find us in."

"His limo?"

"You know about that?"

"Sure. They offer transport to and from the airport and all around the area for tourists coming in, and they rent it out for weddings or other special occasions. It's a nice income supplement to the tourist angle of their ranching business." She stepped toward him. "But I hate to take the limo from them. What if something happens and we wreck it? We're not exactly the safest people right now."

"Not another word!" Amy's brisk tone came from behind Rogan, who turned toward the older woman. She poked her graying head through the door, and her gaze inspected Trina up and down. "I wish I could tuck you right into bed for the good rest that you need, but it doesn't look like that's an option. At least in the limo you can stretch out comfortably in the back…that is, if this guy is up to driving." She shifted her attention toward Rogan.

"Volunteer chauffeur here." He raised a hand, palm out. "But we need to get going, Trina." His gaze lasered into her.

She nodded and allowed him to usher her out into the hallway with a hand on her lower back, as if ready to catch her if she collapsed. As she trod toward the Millers's front door, a lump grew in her throat. Once she stepped into that limousine, she was leaving behind everything dear to her for who knew how long. Yet she couldn't stay here and continue endangering her friends.

Trina turned toward Jim, who stood gazing at them, brow furrowed.

"After we're clean away," she said to her friend, "would you call in an anonymous tip and make sure someone checks for the sheriff and the snowplow driver at the plow garage? The cartel leader said he left them there unconscious."

Jim nodded. "Will do. I have no doubt the state police and possibly even the feds will be swarming into the area. You just let Rogan here get you safely into the marshals' custody, and we'll be happy."

"Keep as much distance as you can from all this," Rogan said. "Don't draw attention to yourselves, or you could expect a hostile visit if certain people think you might know something about where we went."

"We'll be careful." Amy nodded. "The limo is stocked with sandwiches, chips and beverages. Help yourselves."

"The gas tank is full," Jim added, "and Rogan and I made sure your firearms are fully loaded and you've got plenty of extra ammo. I hope you don't have to use any of it."

Trina gulped against the sob that tried to crowd into her throat. "You're dear friends. I hate to ask more of you, but when it's safe, would you go to my place and look after my animals?"

"No problem," Tom said. "We'll bring them here until you get back."

"And Chica, too." She turned toward the dog, who sat on her haunches near the door, eager gaze latched upon her. "Stay." She wagged a finger toward the animal, who whimpered a soft protest but settled onto her belly and laid her muzzle on her paws.

Trina accepted the clean, dry parka offered to her by Amy and allowed the woman to help her slip into it and then fashion a makeshift sling for the arm made from a large white towel. The support brought instant relief to her shoulder. Amy held her boots while she slid her feet into them, then the woman calmly tucked Trina's pistol in the rear of her waistband.

"Shall we?" Rogan asked, opening the kitchen door.

Jaw tensing, Trina hefted her shotgun, nodded and stepped outside onto the porch. The wind had died to a zephyr, but the air was frigid enough to pinch her cheeks. The limo stood, engine purring, at the base of the porch steps.

With a hand on her elbow, Rogan helped her down the steps and into the spacious passenger compartment of the limousine. The area held a pair of padded lounge chairs at the rear, parallel couches along either side and a jump seat in front of the partition between passengers and driver. The top half of the partition was glass and featured a large rectangular window that could slide open and shut. A console running up and down the central area held a miniature refrigerator, a television and a stereo system. Trina sank onto one of the couches. Curling into a ball of misery held a certain pitiful appeal.

"Stretch out and grab a nap if you want," Rogan

said then closed the door on the chill and climbed into the driver's seat.

A soft click and slight lurch forward indicated him putting the vehicle into Drive. A tiny jerk and a soft click indicated he'd quickly halted the limo.

"We've got company."

Rogan's taut tone zinged Trina to attention. She sat forward and peered ahead through the glass of the partition and the windshield. Her heart turned a dizzying somersault. A trio of dark SUVs had come to a halt, nose to tail, on the partly plowed highway, blocking the exit from the Millers' driveway. Several pulse beats thudded through Trina's veins, and then two of the vehicles proceeded on down the road. The third turned and headed up the driveway. If past experience provided any clue, as many as five armed-to-the-teeth thugs were headed straight toward them. So much for making a clean getaway or keeping Jim and Amy clear of danger.

"God, help us," she whispered as Rogan lifted the rifle from the passenger seat beside him.

Rogan narrowed his gaze on the looming enemy vehicle. There wasn't going to be much strategy going into this fight. From his brief acquaintance with Jim, he had a feeling the guy would back his play with whatever weapons were in the house, but Jim and Amy were civilians who might never have fired on a human being, much less on ruthless crooks who would be slinging hot lead right back at them. Rogan ground his teeth together. No matter what, they were almost certainly outmanned and outgunned. Whichever way this went, it was going to be quick and dirty.

"Get down," he told Trina over his shoulder.

"Open the partition window and slide through it," she hissed at him. "The outer windows are too dark for anyone to see inside, so they don't know we're here. Jim's coming out of the house, unarmed and with an aw-shucks grin on this face. He's going to bluff. We need to hide in case someone decides to poke their noses through the door to check the interior. There are two pockets of space back here in the far corners between the ends of the couches and the lounge chairs. We'll just have to fold ourselves into them."

Ignoring the sharp complaints from the wound in his side, Rogan shimmied over the seat into the passenger compartment. Then he followed Trina to the back. She was right about the hiding places, but it was going to be some trick for them to stuff themselves out of sight. Yet, what had to be done had to be done.

"Hi, folks. What can I do for you?"

Jim's jovial greeting to the intruders barely carried to Rogan's ears through the high-end vehicle's soundproofing as he worked himself, the rifle and his handgun into the limited space. He'd noted that Trina was clutching her pistol as well as her shotgun. Anyone who rooted them out of their burrows was going to get a warm welcome.

"Just stopping by to take a look at this interesting vehicle," a gruff voice answered. "Who'd call for a limousine before the snow is cleared after a blizzard?"

"Fresh powder draws in the skiers like bees to

honey. And you know those executive types. They *do* like to travel in style."

Rogan nodded to himself. Props to Jim for sounding 100 percent natural. Probably because he was stating simple truths.

"Airport run, then?" The stranger's voice grew louder, which meant the guy was walking closer.

"What's a group of guys like you doing out in the boonies right after a snowstorm?"

At Jim's mildly aggressive counter-question, the hair at the nape of Rogan's neck prickled.

"Mind if I take a look inside?" The voice was right at the passenger door.

"Knock yourself out," Jim answered even as the door yanked open, admitting a draft of cold air that tickled Rogan's nose.

He held his breath, feeling but not seeing the flinty gaze of the hard case checking out the interior of the vehicle. At last, the intruder grunted, and the door slammed shut.

"Have a nice day." The goon's words were too frosty to be sincere, but at least the sound was fading as if the guy was retreating.

"Check us out on our website." Jim's voice was raised like he was calling after someone. "Our rates are posted. We're real reasonable."

A vehicle door slammed, and an engine revved. Then the vehicle noise trailed away into nothing.

"Trina?" Rogan called softly. "I think they left."

"Yeah."

Her voice came out cracked and faint, whether from

relief or from the pain her scrunched position must be causing her, he couldn't tell. Probably both.

Gritting his teeth, he began wriggling out of his cramped quarters. If his stitches didn't tear again, it would be amazing. He got free in time to spot Jim entering the passenger compartment. The man headed toward Trina, who was moaning as she attempted to unwind herself and gain her feet. Rogan went to help, and between the two of them, they soon had her stretched out on one of the couches. Healthy color had leached from her face. Rogan touched her forehead. It was clammy.

"I'm fine," she gritted out. "Just stressed. I don't think I'm bleeding again, so if you're not, either, we'd best get on our way."

Rogan unzipped the snowsuit and stuck an arm inside. The wound ached and stung, but his palm came away dry.

"I'm fine," he said, holding out his hand toward Jim, who hovered nearby, frowning down at Trina. "You're a good man," he said as they exchanged a firm shake. "Let me know if I can ever return the favor."

The rancher let out a tight chuckle. "I hope not. I'm going to work really hard at never needing help to go on the run from a drug cartel."

"You do that."

Less than a minute later, with a sandwich and a bottle of water keeping him company in the chauffeur's seat, Rogan turned the long vehicle out onto the highway and finally allowed himself a deep breath.

"It actually works in our favor that those goons

checked out the limo before we even left the yard," he said. "These guys communicate, so now none of Statham's men will suspect the limo. I'm going to head toward the US marshals' office in Casper, where my friend is posted. He'll be able to help you get out of sight and stay there until this is over."

No response came from his passenger in the rear, so he glanced over his shoulder through the glass partition. Trina's lithe form was stretched along a cushy leather couch. She lay still with her eyes closed, her long lashes brushing her cheeks. Sound asleep. Just what the doctor would have ordered if she'd been able to see one.

Rogan smiled and turned his attention back toward the unfolding highway that winter's touch had made more a ribbon of white than asphalt gray. In a few hours, he could get on with his mission, assured of Trina's safety, though not without deep regret that he'd inadvertently caused this tectonic shift in her life. Hopefully, one day she'd be able to get back on track and find normalcy again. If Trina was a smart, gutsy powerhouse in the face of the extraordinary challenges they'd just come through, she must be an effortless force of nature in her everyday life.

Too bad he couldn't look forward to being around to observe the doc in her element, as undeniably fascinating and attractive as she was. His survival was anything but assured, and if he somehow made it through this mess, he had his career with the DEA to think about. A success with this undercover assignment—long shot that it had now become—would assure him the ability to pick his next post of duty. Ever since he'd started with the agency, he'd had his eye on a permanent posting in a major metro—East or West Coast didn't matter. Any place where he could put down roots—finally. Where the real action was found. The boonies of Wyoming didn't make the cut.

Rogan shook his head and rolled his shoulders. Best keep his mind on the immediate business if he wanted to survive to see dreams come true.

By the time the county road finally connected with a state highway, they were down out of the mountains onto the high plains, and travel conditions improved. They began to make good time. Soon he started to see road signs for Casper. When they were less than an hour out, he pulled into the parking lot of a large truck stop, not as much to top off the gas tank, which he did, but more to pick up a burner cell so he could phone his buddy in the marshals' service. By the time he returned to the vehicle to make his call, Trina was sitting up and eating one of the sandwiches Amy had packed.

"How are you doing?" he asked as he slid into the driver's seat.

A small smile flickered across her lips. "Better than expected, which isn't nearly as bad as it could be."

A shiver ran down Rogan's spine at the thought of what would have happened had the bullet hit her a few inches to the right and found her heart rather than her shoulder. "Which means," he said, "bad as things are, we can still be thankful."

Her soft laugh brightened the atmosphere. "A man of faith, are you?"

"Sometimes." He began pecking numbers into the burner phone. "Faith is hard to hang on to when you're in deep cover."

"I would think light might be the most important thing to cling to when you're in darkness."

"Yep—doesn't mean it's easy."

"I know what you mean."

The depth of feeling in her words struck a chord in Rogan, but this was not a good time to explore emotions—his or hers. Best if he spent his time prepping her to be as comfortable as possible with their next move.

"I'm going to call Deputy Marshal Ethan Ridgeway now," he told her. "He's a good guy. We met in college when we took criminal justice classes together. After we graduated, he headed for US Marshals' Service basic training camp in Georgia while I went to Quantico to train as a DEA agent, but we've stayed in touch over the past decade while we've been pursuing our law enforcement careers in different agencies."

"Even while you've been undercover?" She canted her head at him.

He nodded. "Yes, even these past three years, I would call him from time to time just to hear a friendly voice who knew the real me. He's aware that I've been undercover someplace in the US, which was why I couldn't meet up with him in person. It may come as a bit of a shock to him to find out we've been in the same state the whole time, but he'll be willing to help."

"We definitely need as much of that as we can get." Her response was emphatic.

He offered her a reassuring smile, but as the call rang through, his gut tightened.

"Deputy Marshal Ridgeway."

Ethan Ridgeway's crisp, competent tone knocked a boulder away from Rogan's chest. He hadn't known how tense he was about successfully getting through to his friend. Now, it was only a matter of making the arrangements.

"Hey, buddy. It's Rogan. I've got a job for you."

"Rogan!" Ethan's voice went low, almost furtive, and footsteps sounded like the man was walking briskly somewhere. Away from company he didn't want to overhear their conversation? "Where are you, man? There's interagency brouhaha going on over you right now like you wouldn't believe."

Rogan's heart fell. "You mean, the law enforcement community in general already knows I'm a blown undercover agent for the DEA? That was fast. I figured it was too soon for the agency to feel desperate enough to reach out to other branches in order to find me. They like to keep a lid on their messes."

"Don't we all." Ethan snorted. "Probably proactive face-saving is why none of us has permission to tell the public your agent status yet. Your agency is going to want to figure out a positive spin on the situation before they claim you as one of theirs. The word is you've gone nuts, blown your cover, got in a gunfight that seriously wounded a civilian and ran off with a million dollars in drug money. I don't buy any of it, but there's a BOLO out on you. You've got to turn yourself in and set the record straight."

The oxygen froze in Rogan's lungs. A be-on-the-lookout issued on him?

If that were true, every law enforcement agency in the country was now authorized to hunt him down, not just the cartel. And who had fed his fellow law enforcement personnel the line about him shooting a civilian and stealing cartel money? Had to be the work of the mole. Claiming that amount of money was missing from cartel coffers was enough to make it appear greed had caused him to betray his agency.

How sneaky and canny to rig it so he'd be the subject of an intense manhunt both inside and outside the law. If the cartel couldn't catch him, he'd be chased down by his own kind. And when he was taken into custody, he'd be a sitting duck for the mole to arrange his death. A slick, easy way to make sure he was silenced for good.

"You're right about me," Rogan told his friend. "I didn't blow my cover. A traitor in the DEA did. And I sure didn't shoot a civilian or run off with cartel money—at least not more than the few thousand I need to stay alive and off the radar until I can prove what's really going on."

Trina's face drew into his line of sight as she moved to the jump seat and leaned close to the partition. Her dark gaze questioned him. He shook his head at her, and a furrow appeared between her eyebrows.

"Come in then," Ethan said. "Tell your story. We'll figure it out."

Rogan sucked in a deep breath. If only he could do that.

"You know my innocence isn't going to be that easy to prove unless I can finger the mole, and I'll be dead within hours of entering custody."

"The marshals' service is better than that. *I'm* better than that. We can protect you. Trust us."

"I *do* trust you. That's why I'm calling. But you know the way things work as well as I do. The marshals' service may not be able to hang on to me. I'm suspected as a rogue DEA agent. An order will come down, the DEA will come collect me and the mole will arrange for a fatality. I'll probably get shot allegedly trying to escape, or they'll rig something to make me look like a suicide."

"If you're not going to turn yourself in, why are you calling?" Ethan's tone was halfway to a snarl. Probably from frustration. But the fact that the man didn't argue with Rogan's logic spoke volumes about his reluctant agreement with Rogan's assessment of the situation.

"There's someone else I need you to protect."

FIVE

Seated in the front passenger seat of the limousine, Trina rubbed her aching arm. They'd been sitting in this downtown parking garage in Casper, Wyoming, for the past twenty minutes waiting for Rogan's contact to show up. The winter cold was beginning to invade the interior, but they couldn't afford to run the engine and betray their position. Somehow, Rogan had managed to back the long vehicle into a space between a long-box pickup truck and an extended Suburban, shielding all but the limo's front end. Trina's gaze scanned the dimness, but other than a few vehicles, there had been no significant movement in the vicinity.

"I don't like this," Trina said—not for the first time in the two hours since Rogan got off the phone with Ethan Ridgeway. Rogan had promptly ditched the burner phone after using it, so they had no way to call and find out if the deputy marshal was on schedule.

Rogan frowned at her—not for the first time, either, in the past two hours. "I don't see any other way to get you to safety. I know the handoff plan's not perfect, but—"

"You're going to get yourself caught. And even if you don't and this Ethan fellow successfully hauls me into protective custody, how sure are you that the marshals' service is going to be able to hang on to me? You didn't think they'd be able to maintain custody of *you*."

"Different ballgame." He shrugged. "I'm a suspected perpetrator and a law enforcement agent to boot. You're a civilian witness. Protecting civilian witnesses is the purview of the marshals' service. They'll have dibs, and I trust Ethan. He assured me he'd handle your case personally."

Trina sent him a sharp look. "I hate to point this out, but you trusted the people in your agency, too. Look where that's gotten you." Her heart panged at being so blunt about a subject that had to be raw for him, but this was no situation for tact.

Rogan let out a guttural sound like a cross between a growl and a whine. "Once I know you're as safe as you can possibly be under these circumstances, I plan to contact my DEA handler who works out of the Casper office."

"Couldn't he or she be the mole?"

"He. Name's Jay Reynolds. If he were in the cartel's pocket, why wait until now to suddenly expose my identity?"

"Good point."

"But I haven't ruled him out. Maybe there was a reason for keeping me in play out there as long as I was, but I consider that possibility unlikely. I won't let him take me in—at least not yet—but I have a few questions for him. The answers could point me toward the culprit." As he spoke, he stared out the window, his eyes busily scanning, like her own.

"Are you sure you can't handle this from within the system?" she asked. "Do you *need* to stay on the run?"

"Yes." His tone was terse.

"Fine. But it sounds like you're planning to do whatever it is you need to do all on your own. Don't you need help?"

His head swiveled toward her, his gaze piercing. "Are you volunteering? Like I'd let you!"

Trina opened her mouth, but no sound came out. *Was* she volunteering?

This guy had barged into her life, gun in hand, bringing all sorts of danger with him. His actions had uprooted her from her home and her practice. She should be eager to escape his company, but for some incomprehensible reason, she wasn't. In the blink of an eye, it seemed, she'd come to care what happened to him—almost as if she had assumed some responsibility for his well-being. Maybe such near-instant comradery came with the territory of first having him for a patient and then fighting beside him for survival. Was this the sort of bonding Dad and Rick had talked about happening between their buddies and them in the war zone?

Of course, the phenomenon had nothing to do with the unwelcome fact that she found him appealing as a man. Since Rick had been killed eight years ago, she'd sworn off guys in dangerous occupations. But maybe sticking to her vow was why she'd stopped dating altogether. Sheer boredom with her choice of companions. Why, oh, why, did she always gravitate toward the John Wayne types?

But uncomfortable self-examination was going to have to wait. Something—no, someone—was moving out there in the dim bowels of this parking level. A shadowy figure was walking up the ramp toward them, exactly the way Rogan had requested his friend to make the approach, on foot.

"We're in business." Rogan tapped her on the knee. "Like we discussed, you get out quietly and tuck yourself into the ell near the stairway. I'll move to a vantage point behind that van over there." He pointed toward a nearby vehicle with a company logo on the side. "I'll be watching with this—" he patted the rifle "—until I'm sure my buddy has taken you safely into custody. Then I'm going to have to disappear."

"Gotcha." She put her hand on the door latch. "When I can, I'll call Jim and Amy and let them know where to pick up their fancy ride."

"Better let me do that. If you do it, the marshals' service will know about this vehicle, and they'll have to impound it for forensic examination. Then the DEA will be all over Jim and Amy for helping us—er, me."

"Not to mention the angry cartel." Trina's gut twisted. The last thing she wanted was to get her friends in trouble for being good neighbors.

"Leave your pistol here," Rogan said. "And the shotgun. Ethan wouldn't be happy to find you packing, and it would delay the proceedings if he has to disarm you before whisking you away."

She opened her mouth to protest but closed it and set her handgun on the console between them then propped the shotgun on the floor against her seat. Clutching her shoulder bag—the only personal item remaining to her—she exited the vehicle. Her gaze darted here and there as she assessed the distance between her and the ell where she was to meet the deputy marshal. Rogan had parked in a position that allowed her to reach the ell without breaking cover. The man's constant and accurate planning revealed his level of intellect at the same time as it betrayed the acute paranoia he'd been forced to develop in order to stay alive.

Trina moved as quickly and quietly as possible to her position behind a section of wall shielding the stairwell door. Her breath emerged in staccato puffs of white as the steady *tap, tap, tap* of footsteps drew closer to where she hid. An inner chill raised the hairs on her arms and neck.

Please, God, this needs to go well.

The footsteps stopped. Trina's pulse thundered in her ears, and she scarcely dared draw a breath.

"Deputy Marshal Ethan Ridgeway," said a strong tenor voice. "Rogan, you out there?"

"I-it's me. Trina Lopez." She bit her lower lip.

Where had that tremulous tone come from? So not herself. But then, she'd never been in a situation like this before.

"Where are you, Ms. Lopez?"

"The stairway ell."

"I'm coming to you." The footsteps resumed.

Soon, a tall, lean man with straw-colored hair and

piercing hazel eyes strode into view. He approached to within half a dozen feet of her. His marshals' service jacket was reassuring. He appeared to be who he said he was. Trina relaxed marginally. But she must still have resembled a deer in the headlights, because the man stopped and lifted his hands, palms out.

"You can trust me," he said. "We're going to keep both of you safe."

"Both of us?"

"Rogan!" the marshal called, head swiveling as his gaze scanned the area. "I know you must be nearby. I couldn't do this off the books. I *had* to report the situation to my agency. The garage is surrounded by marshals and local PD. No DEA. You need to let us take you into custody."

"I knew you'd have to report my call." Rogan's voice echoed through the cavernous space, making it difficult to pinpoint his exact location. "I wouldn't have it any other way. I was never asking you to endanger your career. Go ahead and get Trina out of here and let me worry about slipping through your dragnet."

Marshal Ridgeway muttered something angry under his breath. "Come on, buddy. Don't be stubborn and stupid. Let's *all* live through this. I—"

The sound of multiple vehicle doors popping open drowned whatever else the marshal was going to say. The fusillade from automatic weapons spun Rogan's friend around and slammed him to the concrete.

Trina screamed and dug into her purse. She came out with the small Smith & Wesson Shield semiautomatic she always carried. Rogan had never asked her if she had a gun in her handbag. Probably because she was carrying other weapons right out in the open. Now, she was very glad she hadn't volunteered the information or caved completely to his request to leave all her firearms in the limo.

Men with guns swarmed toward her location. She peered around the retaining wall that offered her partial protection, took aim and cut the knee out from under one of the assailants. The guy shrieked and went down. Bullets splatted into the cement block wall near her head, and she ducked back. Several yards away, a rifle boomed, and another attacker bit the pavement. Rogan. The rest scattered for cover behind various vehicles.

Marshal Ridgeway struggled to a seated position against the retaining wall. He pulled out his service weapon and held it at the ready, though from the bloodstain spreading across the front of his jacket, he wouldn't be able to assist with defense for very long before he passed out. Plus, he was exposed on the far side of the wall. With a sharp cry, Trina knelt, grabbed the man's jacket and pulled him into the marginal cover of the ell.

Ripping open his jacket and then his shirt, she peered at the wound slightly to the right of his breastbone. He was bleeding profusely, but not spurting, nor was there a gurgle in his breathing. The bullet hadn't hit an artery or the lung, then. This man could live if he received prompt medical attention. Too bad a renewed fusillade of bullets reduced the chances of that happening. Trina yanked the winter scarf from around her neck and pressed it against the wound.

Ridgeway's hand closed on top of hers. "I can hold the scarf. You and Rogan concentrate on defending yourselves until the cavalry arrives. The gunfire is going to draw them in from the perimeter in a hurry."

"This attack is from the cartel, then?"

Trina flinched at another spate of automatic weapon fire pinging into cars and shattering glass, followed by a sharp answer from Rogan's rifle.

The marshal grimaced. "Has to be. Someone must have tipped them off that you'd be in this garage. Only they wouldn't have known which vehicle you'd be in or where exactly in the garage until we all moved or spoke. Guess Rogan was right about a mole somewhere, but I thought my people weren't going to inform the DEA about this meeting until we had the two of you safely in custody."

"Which makes you worry about the integrity of your own agency." Trina finished the unspoken thought for him.

"More likely someone higher up got nervous about not informing the DEA before we took action and made a phone call they shouldn't have."

Trina shook her head. "Maybe so, but I'm sorry. I'm not going to be able to entrust myself to the marshals' service."

Yet how was she going to get out of here? Sure, she could dart through the door beside her and down the stairs, but she'd surely meet law enforcement charging upward toward the battle, and they'd grab her. Besides, she couldn't abandon this wounded man until she knew help had arrived for him. Then, if they survived the cartel attack, she and Rogan would be well and truly caught. Rendered helpless to defend themselves against a deadly threat hidden within the very agencies sworn to serve and protect. Trina's heart squeezed in on itself. Futility had never felt so real.

"We need to get out of here." Rogan darted into the already crowded stairway ell.

Trina's head jerked upward, her eyes wide on him. Ethan's, too, though he moved sluggishly.

Rogan squatted by his friend. "Sorry I got you into this, buddy."

"Not your fault. Something stinks around here...and it isn't you. Go on! Take off! I'll be too unconscious to tell them which way you went."

"I can't leave..." Rogan let his voice trail away as his friend's body went limp.

Trina touched the side of his neck. "There's a pulse."

Shouts and running feet from the stairwell and the interior of the garage heralded the impending arrival of law enforcement from multiple directions, which would mean imminent help for Deputy Ridgeway. Vehicle doors slamming and engines revving indicated the cartel members preparing to flee.

Rogan grabbed Trina's hand. "This way."

He pulled her through the door of the stairway and pointed upward. Together, they scurried up the stairs, their footfalls drowned out by the din of shouts, gunshots, pelting feet and screeching tires.

"We need to get out of this parking garage ASAP," he told Trina as he ushered her out of the stairwell and onto the next floor up from where the gun battle now raged between law enforcement operatives and cartel members. "Trying to corral Stathem's goons will keep the cops and agents distracted for the next few minutes before they start scouring the building for us, but we need to be well away by then."

"How?" Brows lifted, she blinked at him. "I doubt there's a helicopter waiting for us on the roof."

"We'll have to pull a fast one with the elevator." He headed for the elevator doors.

"Won't they have someone stationed down below to intercept anyone coming out?"

Her voice sounded directly on his heels. She might have reservations about his plan, but she was following him anyway.

"Probably, yeah." He hit the button. "But there's a possibility they don't have much personnel to spare with that firefight going on."

She shrugged as the doors slid open and they stepped into the elevator car. "Guess we'll take our chances. Hopefully we won't be shot on sight."

"I have no plans to get either of us shot…again."

He flipped the stop switch on the control panel then reached up, dislodged the roof hatch and shoved it to the side. His stitches pulled with the motion, and he winced. He leaned his rifle against the elevator wall, then, making a foot cradle with his hands, he jerked his head upward toward the opening.

"If I give you a boost, you should be able to crawl up there, even with your bum arm."

"It's not like I have an option." She winced and stepped into his palms.

Several grunts, groans and yelps from both of them later, and she'd reached the roof of the car. Rogan released the stop switch and then handed her the rifle. Puffing slightly from painful exertion, he soon squatted beside her in the metallic-smelling darkness as the car glided downward. A lurch followed by a *ding* announced them stopping. Just below, doors whooshed open.

"Don't move," a sharp female voice cried out.

Rogan pictured the agent or officer stepping up and scanning the empty interior of the elevator car, gun extended.

"No one here," the woman cried.

"Hit the stop button so the car stays on the ground floor," answered a more distant voice. "We need to give them a hand up there. Sounds like a mess. We'll follow the roadway to intercept any retreating suspects."

A click sounded and then retreating feet.

As silently as possible, Rogan let himself down into the elevator car and then helped Trina reach the floor. Pistol in one hand, rifle in the other, he peered into the open area outside the elevator. The pair of booths to process exiting vehicles stood only a few feet away. No personnel were inside. Beyond the booths, chilly air wafted toward them from the street. No one was in sight, but an empty police car sat sideways across the exit. He and Trina were far from home free. With every passing second, more law enforcement would be gathering outside, surrounding them.

"Come on." He motioned with his gun then led the way across the driveway toward a pedestrian exit. Frowning, he stopped at the door. "If only we had a distraction..."

A screech of tires and squeal of brakes, as well as a spate of gunfire, sounded nearly on top of them. Rogan grinned. One distraction coming up. A black SUV, no doubt carrying fleeing cartel members, whooshed past them, barreling toward the vehicle exit and not slowing for the meter arm in its way or the police car in front of it. The bulky SUV shattered the meter arm and then slammed into the car, spinning the smaller vehicle away in a screech of metal and the odor of burning rubber. Shouts and gunshots greeted the smashup. Rogan hit the bar on the door and stepped out onto the sidewalk. As hoped, all personnel were scurrying to stop the escaping vehicle. No one was looking in their direction.

He unzipped his snowsuit and quickly tucked the rifle inside then stuffed his handgun in the waistband of his jeans. She followed suit in tucking her handgun away inside her purse. No wonder she'd been keeping such a tight hold on that bag. He should have known she'd be a concealed-carry woman. Grabbing Trina's hand, he led them away from the battle.

Their feet crunched on occasional snow patches as they passed between low-slung businesses alternating with tall brick office buildings. Soon they merged into little knots of people gathering on the sidewalk at a safe distance to gawk at the conflict taking place in the heart of downtown Casper. The hitch in Trina's breathing let Rogan know she was in pain, but she wasn't letting it slow her down. Hopefully the renewed bleeding from his side wound, indicated by fresh warmth, would not become profuse enough to show through his outerwear.

"Where to now?" she asked.

"Greyhound bus station on I-25."

"Won't buses be one of the first means of transportation law enforcement and the cartel will check for us?"

"I didn't say we were going to ride one, just buy tickets."

"Nice! Misdirection."

Rogan hailed a taxi, and they were off to pretend to take a bus.

"I'm sorry about your friend," she murmured to him as the cityscape whizzed past on either side of them.

"Me, too."

"I hope he's going to be all right."

"Ethan's tough as nails. By now he's probably giving the EMTs a hard time."

A slight smile eased the tension around her mouth, but she kept her gaze straight ahead. He shouldn't be doing it, but for several heartbeats, he admired her elegant profile then forced his attention to return to their surroundings. Traffic patterns seemed normal, and no sirens in the vicinity indicated law enforcement pursuit. That status couldn't last long. If he didn't already feature on every agency's most wanted list, he surely would now.

Maybe he should skedaddle out of the country with Trina. And then what? Consign them both to living as fugitives for the rest of their days? A sour taste entered his mouth. No, from childhood he'd had a bellyful of living on the move, dwelling in shadows, never putting down roots. He'd fought hard to leave all that behind. Besides, he'd blasted into this innocent woman's world and exploded her life. He needed to do anything and everything to give it back to her.

Maybe they could scoot down to Mexico, and he could stash her somewhere safe and then return to the States to work on clearing his name and taking down the cartel, the mole and the shadow boss. When things had gone this far, nothing less than a complete take-down would guarantee Trina's safety. Or his.

"Don't try to sideline me," she said, as if hearing his thoughts. She turned narrowed eyes on him. "Since handing me off to the marshals' service is now officially nixed, I'm in this for the long haul. Face it, I'm your only ally. Let's get this job done."

Rogan opened his mouth. If he could argue with her reasoning, he would.

He shut his mouth.

SIX

"Did they teach you this stuff at the DEA?" Trina asked her companion as they made their way stealthily between tracks in a Burlington Northern Santa Fe train yard. "Or did you go to spy school to learn evasive maneuvers?"

They'd been to the bus station and bought tickets to Boise, Idaho, then promptly left the station and walked to the nearest city bus stop. They rode the bus to a nearby Salvation Army Thrift Store, where Rogan efficiently grabbed items off the racks and outfitted them in new clothing—complete with thick jackets, face-concealing knitted hats, gloves and warm scarves. Then another city bus had taken them to a convenience store, where he purchased bottled water, energy bars and a new burner phone. Finally, a taxi had deposited them near the train yard.

At her lame attempt at humor, she expected a mild chuckle from Rogan, but instead she got a pained grimace and a sour grunt.

"Let's just say my upbringing was not—ah…traditional. One of the reasons I was picked for undercover work. They figured I stood a better than average chance of succeeding in a murky environment."

"Sounds like a story there, but I won't pry."

"I appreciate that." Rogan offered her a slight smile. "But let's hop one of these trains, get settled and then I'll fill you in. I owe you transparency."

They took a few more steps, then his hand shot out. She bit back a yelp as he grabbed her good arm and yanked her into cover behind one of the rail cars. He held her close to himself, his warm breath brushing her cool cheek. Heart hammering against her rib cage, she went very still.

Voices—one male, one female—drew closer, footsteps crunching on the loose gravel lying between the rail lines. She'd noted before what good hearing Rogan possessed. He'd picked up on these people's approach before she did.

"No sign of the fugitives here," the woman said as she and her companion passed only feet from them.

"Nah," answered the man. "Didn't expect so. I heard on the police scanner the main search is concentrated at the truck stops. They'll get 'em. I..."

The voice faded away, and the crunch of footsteps went faint.

The tension in Rogan's body eased, and Trina allowed herself a full breath. He released her, and she stepped back. The wintry air enveloped her, and she shook herself—inwardly and outwardly. Rogan's arms had felt way too comfortable for her peace of mind. She gazed around, head swiveling this way and that.

The distant parking lot in front of the large two-story brick station building was about half-full of vehicles, probably belonging to employees who worked in the offices inside.

"Do you think some agency or the cartel might be staking this place out?"

Rogan shook his head. "I'm sure there's a massive hunt going on for us throughout the city, and all the roads probably have checkpoints. But like that railroad bull said, the long-haul truckers are catching the brunt of the attention."

"Railroad bull?"

"Bull is the slang term for train station cop."

"Oh, like highway bull for highway patrol cop."

"Exactly."

One track over, a train lurched and began to move.

Rogan grabbed her hand. "Let's get aboard, and I'll explain why the authorities will be concentrating on the truckers in their search for us."

Together they ran for the nearest boxcar in motion. Rogan released her hand and shoved at the side door, creating an opening barely big enough to slip inside. He tossed his rifle through the gap. The train continued to gain speed. As Trina scrambled to keep up, Rogan dived into the car, then turned and grabbed her reaching hand. With one great heave, she found herself yanked into the dim interior of a train car that must recently have held lumber. The woodsy odor was distinctive.

The car was now, thankfully, empty, but it was cold, with a dank sort of chill that would soon seep into the bones if they were forced to hunker down in here for any length of time. Rogan's insistence on the heavy outerwear from the Salvation Army made extra sense now. He must have known the environment they were going to be facing.

The door rumbled shut, enclosing them in pitch blackness. Then a light came on, emanating from his new burner phone. He'd bundled his scarf around his neck and lower face and pulled his stocking cap low on his forehead and over his ears. His dark eyes gleamed at her between the knitted folds. Trina followed suit, bundling head and face. Her wounded shoulder ached ferociously. The cold was only going to make the ache worse. She rubbed the spot with a glove-clad hand.

"Come here." Rogan motioned her toward the front of the car and sat down with his back against the wall. He opened his arms to her. "We're going to have to cuddle for warmth."

She understood the rationale, but that didn't mean she had to like it. The only problem was that she *did* like it. Not that she'd tell *him* that. Without a word, Trina settled in close to him.

"Now," he murmured in her ear, "let me tell you the short version of a story about a little boy who lost his mama when he was five years old and then went on the road with his trucker daddy for the next decade of his life."

"Wow," she murmured back. "That does qualify as untraditional."

"It was. Not entirely unhappily so, but a bit rootless

and friendless, except for CB radio buddies I made along the road."

"What about school?"

"Technically, I was homeschooled, but Dad wasn't much on formal education. A lady truck driver named Pinky Spikes oversaw most of my studies."

"Again, over the CB?"

"Pretty much. Occasionally we'd meet up somewhere along the road at a truck stop. The first time I saw her in person, I discovered that her CB handle was intended literally. She had a head full of pink hair that she kept short and spiked."

Trina's laugh came out muffled through her scarf. Their cuddling was working. Everything but her rear end, where it met the cold floorboards, was staying reasonably warm.

"Was she a good tutor?" she asked.

"Seriously excellent. The woman was brilliant. She could have been a college professor if she'd wanted a life off the road."

"Apparently, she did good work with you."

"In more ways than one. I wasn't listening too well at the time, but she was the first one to ever talk seriously to me about God. She planted some good seeds for later, I guess."

"I like her a lot even though I've never met her." Trina pulled her knees up closer to her chest. "I would imagine your DEA file has a record of your unusual upbringing. That's why they're concentrating the search for us at truck stops? They figure you'll default to catching a ride with a familiar mode of transportation?"

"Spot-on." He chuckled. "I was counting on their knowledge of my background as well as the bus ruse as a double distraction from searching the train lines. Good thing for us, I never thought it necessary to include in my personal history on my DEA application the six months Dad and I spent riding the rails after his truck was repossessed. I'd just turned ten. Needless to say, I missed school during that time, but I got an education of another kind, hobo-style. Rail hopping was a fun kind of life—at least for a while. Met a lot of colorful characters, but some of those characters were dark. Very dark."

"Meaning?"

Silence answered her for long seconds, then his shrug communicated to her through the back of her jacket.

"One of the guys we started traveling with was an ex-con. He got in touch with some of his old criminal buddies and they got Dad into trucking again, but this time it wasn't honest work. I think I knew that the whole time, but I pretended not to realize the meaning of all the furtive behavior and unusual places and times for pickups and drop-offs. When I was fifteen, Dad got arrested and went to prison. I was less than shocked. Spent the rest of my underage years in foster care with a decent family."

"So, that meant you started attending school in an actual building?"

"Yup. Went to church with them regularly, too."

"That had to be a huge life change. Did you enjoy settled living?"

"Not at first. The lifestyle felt too foreign, but it grew on me, and now I crave a place to call home. That was one of the big carrots offered to me if I'd take this undercover assignment—my pick of duty postings afterward where I can get my own place to go home to every day, and my career can take off. I'm thinking a metro office where the action is."

Trina's heart shriveled ever so slightly. Rogan wanted big-city life. Good thing she wasn't falling for this guy, or she could be in a world of hurt. Her roots were rural and ever would be.

Her stomach rumbled, and he let out a small chuckle. His arms dropped from around her, and a little rustling told her he was fishing in his pocket for the energy bars. A little water wouldn't hurt, either. Trina swallowed against a dry throat.

"Here you go." He pressed a bar into one of her hands. "It's unwrapped, so chow it down."

They spent a few minutes consuming their snack and rehydrating. Afterward, Trina gratefully allowed him to pull her back into their snuggled position. The pervasive cold was seeping into her body even through the heavy outerwear.

"You said your dad went to prison," she said, leaning into him. "Is he out now? Do you keep in touch?"

"He's out." The streak of sadness in his tone didn't match his hopeful-sounding words. "Got out the hard and sudden way in a prison fight when I'd just turned eighteen, but I do visit his grave now and then."

"I'm sorry for your loss…sorry I asked. I don't mean to be prodding sore spots."

"No worries."

They rode in silence for a time then Trina huffed. "I just have to ask. After all that mess with your dad, what made you want to become an officer of the law, and a DEA agent specifically?"

"Good question." Rogan's tone held a hint of a laugh. "The folks my dad worked for were drug runners. *They're* the ones who ruined my dad's life, not the cops who arrested him or the judge and jury who put him behind bars. I want to do everything I can to take down as many of the drug producers, runners and suppliers as possible."

"I can respect that."

"I'm glad."

This guy was interesting, intelligent, brave and good. Too bad her own personal vow to swear off guys in dangerous jobs, as well as his goal of a big-city career, put him off-limits for her. With the fading of adrenaline and the rhythmic *clickety-clack* of the boxcar against the rails, drowsiness began to creep over Trina, and she allowed herself to relax in Rogan's arms.

"Trina!"

Rogan's urgent voice in her ear roused her from slumber. In the blackness of the rail car, it was impossible to tell how long she'd been napping or even whether it was night or day.

"What is it?" she answered.

"We're slowing down. We need to get out of here before we stop at the station, because the bulls swarm all over a train's arrival."

She groaned. "I think parts of my body have gone

to sleep. I don't know how limber I'm going to be." She gulped against a tightening throat. Only a few days ago, the idea of being on the run from people trying to kill her, much less being forced to jump out of a moving train car, had never crossed her mind. But now here she was.

Rogan flicked on the light from his cell phone then set her aside and rose to his feet. He reached down a hand to help her up. Staggering and teetering, stiff in every limb, she finally made it upright. The train did indeed appear to be slowing. Rogan pulled the car door open a couple of feet, admitting a rush of damp, cold air tainted with odors of railroad track metal and diesel fumes. Under a cloudy sky, a westering sun dipped its toes in a horizon of plowed black dirt that awaited the new planting season. Trina wobbled forward and peered out. The embankment was a blur of dirty snow pocked with patches of dead brown grass.

"Not much snow here to pad our fall," Rogan said. "This area must not have been hit so hard with the recent blizzard."

"The high plains doesn't get near the snow that the mountains do."

"I think we're close to Cheyenne."

"Heading south then," she said.

"Yep. If we can make it to the outskirts of Denver, I know of a cabin belonging to a friend where we can hole up and heal."

"And plan."

"Right."

The train braked with a lurch that sent Trina stumbling into Rogan. He caught her easily. If only his arms around her didn't feel so natural and welcome. She forced herself to pull away.

"Time to go," he said. "You first. Poke your head out, spot yourself a decent snowbank and time your jump to hit it."

Trina winced, already anticipating the jolt of the landing, but there didn't appear to be any alternative to this leap of faith. The train was slowing more by the second, closing in on a multitude of outlying buildings fronting a skyline that signified a city looming ever closer.

"Remember to flex your knees as you jump then land, crumple and roll."

Trina awarded him a lopsided smile. "I'm an outdoors woman. I learned how to jump and land practically from toddlerhood."

He grinned and raised his hands, palms outward. "I'll observe and take notes then."

Laughing softly, she turned and peered out of the car. "Here goes." Clutching her purse, she made her choice and then jumped.

"Trina!" Rogan cried out as his traveling companion landed and rolled top-over-tail and then lay still. Heart in his throat, he leaped from the train and hit the cold ground rolling. The abrupt jar and stab of pain from the wound in his side were peripheral distractions for which he spared no time. He hopped to his feet, snatched up the rifle he'd flung out ahead of him and raced back toward the spot where Trina lay sprawled like a rag doll.

As he hit his knees beside her, she stirred and opened her eyes. "Ou-ouch!" The word rasped long and low from her lips.

"Understatement, I'd imagine." He leaned closer, inspecting her up and down. "Can you move?"

"I-I think so." She attempted to sit up, and Rogan lent her an arm.

Tension ebbed from his chest. Trina was all right. Her well-being had come to matter more to him than anything. Surely, that was because he was responsible for her situation. Any other reason—like his unwelcome, but overwhelming attraction to her—was unacceptable, and this was no time to examine wayward feelings.

"What now?" She fixed him with a solemn gaze.

"For the half hour or so until full dark, we take refuge in that shed over there." He pointed to a small clapboard structure about twenty feet away.

Trina snorted. "At least it's not some unsuspecting farmer's barn."

"Very funny. I'm glad that nasty fall didn't knock the sense of humor out of you."

He helped her to her feet, and together they tottered to the meager shelter. A broken padlock hung from a latch hinge on the door, so access to the small building was unimpeded. The structure was bare except for a couple of empty crates that they appropriated as chairs. Chinks in the wall board admitted slivers of waning light that painted golden stripes across their faces.

"I spotted a road due east of here. We'll hoof it there and hope that it soon takes us to some fleabag motel where they'll be glad to take cash and not look at us too closely."

"Then what?"

"Find somewhere to get a decent hot meal, grab some rest and then hop a bus tomorrow for real."

"You have this being-on-the-lam thing down pat."

"It's a unique skill set for a law enforcement agent. I know." He grinned at her. She grinned back, and Rogan's heart performed a funny little jig.

Good thing Trina had no idea how appealing he found her as a woman, as well as a brave and decent human being. Thankfully, she was showing no signs of reciprocating his interest in her. The last complication they needed in this dangerous situation was falling for each other. If he was going to be honest with himself, the woman had made an indelible impression on him. He could easily tumble head over heels, but he couldn't—wouldn't allow that. Even so, no matter where life took him, memory of her would be a precious legacy that he would always carry. But before their inevitable parting, he had to ensure her well-being.

Darkness soon closed in, and with it, a bitter chill. If he wasn't mistaken, her teeth were chattering.

He rose. "Let's go. We'll hug the rail ditch until we find the road. Step carefully."

"Believe me, a sprained ankle is *not* on my agenda."

He took her hand, and they left their meager shelter. Clouds had moved in, obscuring the moon and the stars, making the night very black indeed, but he didn't dare turn on his phone light. Even such a small glimmer could make their presence known. A few minutes of stumbling progress brought them to the narrow, paved county road, not a state highway, which meant much less traffic. In fact, they'd seen none so far.

They stuck to the graveled edge of the road, their feet crunching on brittle ice that thinly coated the rocks beneath. Soon, they came to a farmstead, where a warm glow filtered through curtains on the first floor of the two-story home, indicating that someone was home. One of the windows framed a decorated tree, and outside, the porch rails were festooned with strings of colorful lights. But the showstopper sat in the center of the yard—a manger scene of life-size, full-color figures of Mary, Joseph, three shepherds and baby Jesus in the manger, each lit from the inside. And the scene was also illuminated by a small floodlight that created an ethereal halo around the entire tableau.

In wordless accord, they both stopped and stared. Trina released a deep sigh, and he glanced toward her shadowy figure beside him, hands stuffed in her parka pockets.

"Are you wishing you were home getting ready to celebrate Christmas?"

"The first part yes, second part no."

She started walking again.

"Not a fan of Christmas?" He fell into step.

"I used to be, but this year is different. I'm not a fan of spending Christmas alone."

"I'm sorry...about your father...and your husband,

too. I don't mean to be nosy, but—uh—I'd think guys would be lining up to ask you out."

She let out a sound like a cross between a sharp chuckle and a snort. "My dad was getting a little impatient with me about my pickiness in the dating department. But, sure, he understood what a tough act Richard was to follow."

"Right. War hero."

"No hyperbole there. At his funeral at least half a dozen servicemen and women came up to me with stories about how Rick saved their lives during various missions. The stories made me prouder of my husband than I already was—quite a feat, believe me—but it also hardened my resolve."

"Your resolve?"

"Never again to get involved with a guy in a dangerous occupation."

"Then along comes Rogan McNally." He barked a laugh to throw off the pinch in his gut at her words that excluded him from her eligible bachelor list. "I mean, not that we're *involved*, of course."

"Not romantically, anyway, but I'd say we're involved."

"I'm sorry for getting you into this."

"Stop saying that!" She turned suddenly, blocking his path.

Rogan dug in his heels to keep from plowing into her.

She poked him in the chest with a gloved hand. "You did what you had to do to stay alive by taking refuge in my barn."

Rogan wrapped his hand around the glove pressed against his breastbone. "You didn't have to patch me up."

"Of course I did. I help wounded creatures. It's what I do."

"You could have just turned me over to Stathem's goons when they first arrived—used me as a bargaining chip for your life. They might have gone for the deal. Hauled me away and left you alone."

"And maybe not." She snorted. "Wasn't an option anyway. I'm William Longrider's daughter and a marine's widow. I don't make deals to save my own life that will cost someone else's."

"So, here we are."

"Here we are."

Rogan lifted his arm and pointed past her shoulder. "Let's check out that set of lights up there. I'm thinking convenience store/gas station. The attendant should be able to direct us to the nearest motel."

"And sell us coffee and pizza, I hope."

The prospect of warmth and sustenance fueled their speed, and soon the sign for the convenience store became clear to see, but so did the bad news. A police patrol car sat parked in the lot. Impossible to tell if anyone occupied the vehicle. Were the officers waiting in the car and watching for strangers coming into town, or were they simply out on their regular patrol and had gone inside to grab coffee and a snack?

"I guess this won't be our first stop in Cheyenne," Rogan said.

"Guess not." Trina huffed.

They passed under cover of the shadow of a closed feed store across the street. Several blocks of sticking to the darkness later and faint, tinny music reached Rogan's ears.

"Honky-tonk dead ahead," he muttered to his companion.

"I hear it, too."

"Not likely a cop hangout."

"Nope, but who knows about what other kinds of trouble."

"I'm willing to chance it."

"Me, too," he said as they hurried toward the music. "Hopefully, the patrons will be preoccupied with themselves, and we can slip in under the radar. Let's wrap our scarves around our heads and pull our caps down so that not much of our faces are showing. Nobody is going to think that's odd on a cold night like this."

Trina's chuckle warmed his chilled insides. "I'm already pretty much wrapped like a mummy."

He glanced at her face under a passing streetlight, and only her dark eyes twinkled back at him.

"I'm on your six," he said, as he opened the door of the run-down bar and grill and stood aside for Trina. As he stepped in behind her, heady warmth rolled over him. "There." He motioned toward a booth in a dimly lit corner.

As hoped, the patrons were busy chattering to one another and downing their drinks and burgers. Their entrance warranted only a few glances from those nearest the door who received an unwelcome cold draft. Gaze scanning their surroundings, Rogan followed

Trina to the booth and scooted in, back to a wall and facing out toward the rest of the room. Over the rear of the bar hung a large flat-screen television displaying the highlights of an NFL game. Most eyes were riveted on the screen, which suited Rogan perfectly.

His mouth watered at the enticing scents of grilled food. He could worry about hardening of the arteries later. Now, he was ordering a fat juicy burger sizzled in its own grease. An indifferent waitress came and took their orders, only slightly raising an eyebrow when they both wanted coffees rather than something harder. She came back shortly with steaming mugs.

As Trina excused herself to use the ladies' room, Rogan loosened his scarf, tugged off his gloves and wrapped his chilled fingers around his hot coffee cup. He refused to allow his spine to relax, only partly because of the discomfort of the pistol tucked into his rear waistband and the rifle slung over his shoulder and hidden under his heavy parka. Sudden warmth after an extended period in the cold could do serious damage to his alertness if he allowed his edge to slip.

Trina returned to the booth, and then their burgers and fries arrived. *Inhaled* would be a polite term for the way they gobbled the food—too ravenous even to exchange a word. Popping the last fry into his mouth, Rogan lifted his gaze to the television screen and met his own eyes staring back at him from a photo of himself. His pulse stuttered. He couldn't hear what the commentator was saying, but he could guess.

John Q. Public, please meet the nation's new most

wanted fugitive, Rogan McNally, considered armed and dangerous..

Was a reward being offered for information leading to his capture? Probably, now that his case had gone so high-profile. Had the DEA made his undercover agent status public yet? Doubtful. More likely they were keeping that knowledge close to the vest until they saw how things turned out. Big bureaucracy hated bad press, so until his agency knew better, they'd be disowning and distancing themselves from their supposedly rogue agent and allowing the world to believe that he was a trigger-happy cartel member who stole from his own.

Then Trina's face popped up beside his, and his pulse completely stalled. What were they saying about her? That she was a wanted fugitive also? Or that she was his hostage? Impossible to say, but the two of them needed to get someplace safe and private where they could watch the news and find out. He wanted to know the status of his friend Ethan, too.

Forcing in a deep breath, Rogan elbowed Trina and nodded up at the screen. She turned her head, and the color faded from her face.

"When you went to the ladies' room, did you notice if this place has a back door?" he whispered to her.

"Yes, it does, and I don't think it's fitted with an alarm. In a low-rent place like this, I imagine there are quite a few people who'd like to slip out the back."

"Good. Let's both get up and head for the back like we're going to use the facilities."

Trina nodded. Rogan tossed enough money on the

table to cover their tab and a generous tip then slid out of the booth. Trina led the way up a narrow, dingy hallway toward a door labeled Exit. They slipped outside into an alley, where the cold enveloped them like a false friend they could do without. At least the darkness was a true pal. He ushered Trina past a large, nasty-smelling garbage bin and on toward the street.

An engine suddenly gunned as a big vehicle roared into the narrow alley and screeched to a halt, blocking their path. Nearly blinded by the headlights, Rogan barely discerned the outline of a pair of burly figures piling out of the pickup truck. But he was totally clear about the *snick-snap* of pump-action shotguns ready to do business.

SEVEN

Trina gasped, and her hand went automatically toward the pistol in her purse.

"Don't make a move," one of their assailants barked out.

She froze, darting a glance toward Rogan as her heart hammered her ribs. Standing still and tall, he had raised his hands. She did the same.

The pair stepped closer, backlit by the vehicle headlights. The shotguns in their grips took clear shape, though their facial features remained in shadow. Who *were* these people? They certainly didn't act like law enforcement. Cartel? But that didn't feel right, either. If it were Stathem's men, wouldn't Rogan and she already be dead?

"Very slowly and carefully," said the other man, "between your thumb and forefinger, take out your pistols and set them on the ground."

Rogan unzipped his jacket and complied. Then he zipped up his jacket again. The rifle never made an appearance, and Trina kept her gaze averted from him as she removed the small Smith & Wesson from her purse and set it on the ground. It might be too much to hope that this pair wouldn't find the rifle, but she wasn't going to do anything to draw attention to it.

"Kick them away," the man said.

They did what they were told, and the pistols skittered into darkness.

"Frisk 'em, Deke," said the one who'd ordered them to give up their pistols.

Trina's heart sank. So much for the rifle.

"Why can't you do it, Barry?" said the other man.

"Because I told *you* to do it."

Grumbling under his breath, the one called Deke leaned his gun against the bumper of the pickup and then came toward Rogan and her. She could make out the man's features now. Youngish—maybe midtwenties—but with hard features. He'd been sitting near them in the bar and grill at a table in the company of an older guy with graying hair—presumably the one covering them with the shotgun.

"Don't try anything!" said shotgun guy.

Trina shivered as Deke quickly ran his hands over her torso and up and down her legs. He snatched her shoulder bag and riffled through it, but finding no additional weaponry, he gave it back to her. Then he turned to Rogan. From one coat pocket, Deke pulled Rogan's cell phone. He tucked it in his own jacket then dived his hand back into the same pocket and came out with the box of slugs for the rifle.

"What do we have here?" He shot an evil grin at Rogan. "Let's see what else you've got."

He fished inside the opposite side pocket and pulled out Rogan's wad of cash. With a gleeful laugh, he held the cash and the ammo high for his partner to see. The older man let out a sharp grunt.

"Find the gun that goes with the ammo," he said, "but toss me the dough."

Deke stuck out his lower lip, but the older man repeated the command with a harsh edge to his voice, and the younger man threw the cash roll to him. Barry pocketed it.

The younger man returned his attention to Rogan. "I think the big gun is under his jacket."

"Off with it." Barry motioned with his shotgun.

Rogan unzipped and removed the jacket entirely, exposing the rifle underneath.

"Whoa, man! A Tikka T3X." Deke stripped Rogan of the firearm and rubbed the stock with his palm. "Ain't she a beaut!"

"Quit messing with the rifle," Barry said. "You can buy yourself a whole truckload with what we've got coming."

Deke let out a wild whoop that sent Trina's heart into her throat. "We got 'em, Barry! That fifty-thousand-dollar reward is all ours! We just have to figure out how to hand them off to the cops and collect our payday without getting our own selves pinched."

Trina's mouth went dry. Were these guys more than money-hungry civilians? Were they crooks who didn't dare deal with the police directly?

"Shut up, Deke," Barry snapped. "I ain't after no lousy fifty grand or taking a chance on getting arrested. The news report says this dude stole a cool million. He's going to hand it over to us if he and his woman want to keep on breathing. Ain't that right, Mr. Rogan McNally?"

"Whatever you say, Barry." Rogan's tone was flat calm as he put his jacket back on.

The hairs along Trina's arms prickled. More danger was packed in that cool response than all the heated protests in the world. Did Barry even have a clue?

"Glad you feel that way, McNally. Now, where is it?"

"Hid it, did ya?" said the one named Deke. "Well, you'd better take us to it right now." He reclaimed his shotgun but tucked it under one arm while he pointed the rifle at them.

The pair motioned toward the truck with their weapons. Rogan led the way to the rear of the club cab. Trina stayed close, but not too close in case Rogan needed room to make a sudden move—though what that might be against armed thugs, she had no idea. They reached the truck, and Deke pulled a short length of rope from the truck bed and tied Rogan's hands in front of him then shoved him into the rear seat. Trina started to follow, but a rough hand pulled her back and whirled her around.

"You're driving, missy." Barry stuck his beefy face close to hers. "Deke'll keep his new gun on your boyfriend in the back seat, and I'll have mine on you in the front."

The man's hot breath stank of beer and onions. Wrinkling her nose, Trina climbed into the driver's seat. The diesel engine growled as she put the truck in gear and backed out of the alley.

"Which way, McNally?" the one called Barry demanded.

"Better grab I-80 west toward Rock Springs."

"Rock Springs, eh?" Barry chuckled. "Back toward the scene of the crime, then." He prodded Trina in the side with the barrel of his shotgun and gave her directions to the interstate.

With the tires purring beneath them, Barry snickered. "Your boyfriend tell you what a mess he made in Rock Springs? Big shootout. Bigger than Cheyenne. All over the news. An innocent woman got caught in the crossfire."

Trina's heart squeezed in on itself. Rogan hadn't shared any details of what had occurred to send him on the run. Just that he'd come from Rock Springs. The trip from Rock Springs to Pinedale, the largest town near her ranch, was only a couple of hours' drive. Comfortable journey in a car, but Rogan had been on a motorcycle, wounded and driving through a winter storm in the mountains. She could scarcely think of a situation more miserable, but what was this about a bystander getting shot? She couldn't very well ask right now.

"He's not my boyfriend," Trina said softly.

"Oh, that's right." Deke snapped his fingers in the back seat. "The cops don't know what to think about you. Are you the girlfriend or an innocent hostage?"

"Hostage," Rogan said.

“Riiight!” Deke chuckled. “That’s why you trusted her with a pistol.”

“Think what you want,” Rogan said. “Since you fellows have been paying such close attention to the news reports, any word on how that wounded US marshal from Casper is doing?”

“What do you care?” Barry asked.

“US Marshal Ethan Ridgeway is a friend of mine. I’m an undercover DEA agent.”

Barry hooted. “You just want to know ’cause he’s in critical condition in the hospital, and if he doesn’t pull through, you’re in even worse trouble than you were before. If you’re a fed, then I’m an international spy. Not likely!”

“It’s true,” Trina said. Whatever Rogan was hoping for in exposing the truth about himself, she was going to back him up. “When the cartel came looking for him at my ranch, their leader told me they’d found out Rogan was undercover DEA.”

“What if it’s on the level, Barry?” Deke’s voice quivered slightly. “Maybe this is some kind of sting operation, and we’ve kidnapped a federal agent.”

“Relax, you knothead,” Barry responded. “Even if he *was* DEA, which I’m not saying I believe, he’s gone rogue. They wouldn’t put out a reward on him otherwise. Rogan the rogue, that’s what we have here.” The man swiveled his head and glared into the back seat. “Couldn’t keep your hands out of the cartel cookie jar, could you?”

“Whatever.” That scary, too-calm tone was back in

Rogan's voice. "I'm going to grab a few hours' shut-eye. Let me know when we get there."

Heat flared on Trina's face, and she gritted her teeth. They were in the clutches of gun-toting crooks who were going to be furious when they found out there was no million dollars. And Rogan was going to take a nap? This was taking the cool customer act too far, wasn't it?

Trina inhaled a deep breath and let it out slowly. Her acquaintance with Rogan had been brief, but enough to know he didn't do anything without a reason—usually a very smart reason. If only she knew what that reason was, she'd feel a whole lot more confident. Not that she had any choice but to trust him. He hadn't survived this long as an undercover agent without knowing how to handle himself in sticky situations.

Her churning gut settled back into place. If he could play it cool, she could, too.

Rogan laid his head back against the truck seat and closed his eyes. Ethan was still alive. Good to know. At least he could surmise that much from Barry's mocking response to his question.

As far as his gambit to get their captors at odds with each other over his status as a federal agent, the results hung in the balance. So far, Barry had plowed over his partner's misgivings, but there might be only so much belittling and bossing Deke could take before the pair would be at each other's throats and distracted from Trina and him. Trina… was a quick study, he'd give her that. She'd gone along right away, and she'd move fast when the hoped for time came to make his play. It was a dangerous game, one that could backfire and get them killed, but it was better than doing nothing. If he'd learned anything the past few days, neither of them was wired for passivity.

A click announced the radio coming on. No, not the regular radio—a police band scanner. Must be the portable kind available in lots of electronics stores, because he hadn't seen a scanner installed on the truck's dashboard when he checked the fuel gauge as he climbed inside. These guys were serious about knowing what the cops were up to in the area, confirming his suspicion that Barry and Deke were criminals currently wanted by the law. It might be helpful to know what the pair had done to earn police attention. The chatter seemed mundane. Then a call came in to dispatch from a squad car saying the officers had found an abandoned vehicle that matched the description of one involved in a recent convenience store holdup where a clerk was seriously wounded by a shotgun.

Next to Rogan, Deke squirmed in his seat. Armed robbery sounded about right for these two, and apparently, they weren't shy about shooting. Bad news. But the good news was, if Barry and Deke had been forced to abandon their car after the robbery, this pickup was probably stolen. A call could come in at any time reporting the theft. Then the pair would either need to abandon this vehicle and take another, or else stay on the run and hope the stolen truck wasn't spotted by a sharp-eyed highway bull on I-80. Whatever their captors decided to do in the matter of the stolen truck, his quick glance at the fuel gauge had told him they'd have to stop for gas along about Rawlins, halfway to their destination of Rock Springs.

The wound in his side ached ferociously, and he hadn't had much sleep since the cartel attack at Trina's ranch, but grabbing a nap for real right now was out of the question. He needed to stay alert. Working on loosening the ropes that bound him would help him do that. Curling his fingers back toward his wrists, he probed the knot. It was tied firmly but simply—not impossible to work loose with a little time and patience. He probably had a couple hours of the former, but he was running short of the latter. Too many people were getting hurt to protect the identity of a rat in the DEA and the miserable rodent's shadow boss who masterminded the thriving drug routes through Wyoming.

Rogan kept his ears open while he worked at the knot, but nothing further of interest came through the police band radio, and Trina remained silent behind the wheel. Barry and Deke nattered back and forth about what they were going to do with their "big score." The pair were getting entirely too chummy when Rogan wanted them ready to go for each other's throats. He shifted in his seat and was about to pretend to wake up so he could stir the pot, but a light laugh from Trina stopped him.

"What's so funny?" Barry demanded.

"You two," she said. "I wonder which one of you is going to double-cross the other first. Partners have been known to turn on each other for a lot less than a million bucks."

Rogan allowed himself a small smile under the cover of darkness. Excellent job at stirring up trouble in the paradise building up in these men's small minds. This woman was a gem. They were so much on each other's wavelengths, it was a little bit scary.

"Shut up and drive," Barry snarled at Trina.

Deke lunged forward against his seat belt. "You're telling her to shut up, but you're *not* telling me I shouldn't worry about a double cross?" Apparently, Barry's lack of protest over the implied accusation wasn't lost on the younger partner.

"You zip it, too. I shouldn't have to tell you to trust me." Barry's tone was just frosty enough to come across as insincere. "Stop being an idiot. These two are only trying to rile us."

And it was working. Rogan smirked. Deke subsided, but if it was possible to feel waves of resentment flowing off someone, Rogan was drowning in them.

At last the stubborn knot he was working started to loosen. He opened his eyes in time to glimpse a billboard announcing Rawlins only ten miles ahead. They'd have to pull over for gas soon. A short time later, barely at the edge of the city, the lights of a mega–truck stop appeared ahead.

"We're going to pull in here," Barry said to Trina. "But draw up to a pump as far away from the building as possible."

"All right, but can I get out and stretch my legs, maybe use the facilities?" Trina asked.

"No and no. I'm the only one who's going to get out,

and that's just to pay for the gas with your boyfriend's wad here." Barry held up Rogan's cash roll.

"What if *I* need to use the facilities?" Deke asked.

"Do you?"

"No."

"Then why did you ask?" The older man turned and glared at the younger.

"Because I'm tired of you bossing me around."

"If you're so tired of me, then as soon as we collect our payday from this mope—" Barry jerked his head toward Rogan "—I say we go our separate ways."

"Deal." Deke grinned as Trina stopped the pickup next to an illuminated pump on the far end of the line. "But get me a soda and a bag of corn chips while you're inside paying."

"Nope." Barry shook his head. "If you gobble and guzzle, then a few miles up the road you really *will* have to use the facilities, and we ain't stopping again."

Deke said something foul under his breath. Scowling, Barry tucked his shotgun under his jacket the way Rogan had been carrying the rifle. He lasered a warning glare toward Deke then climbed out of the truck and went to the pump. Rogan sat forward slightly, scanning their surroundings.

"Hey, you, sit still." Deke prodded him in the side with his shotgun and managed to nudge Rogan's wound.

Breath hissed between Rogan's teeth, and his hands involuntarily formed fists. The action spread the loosened ropes enough that it would only be a matter of shaking the bindings off when the time was right to make his move.

"How are you doing, Trina?" he asked. "Having any trouble staying awake?"

"I'm fine, Rogan. No trouble at all."

Good. She was ready for action—as if he'd expected anything less.

"You know they plan to kill us, don't you?"

"I know." The answer came so soft and calm she could have been responding to a question about the weather.

"I ain't no killer." Deke's protest emerged flabby at best.

"No?" Rogan trained a sharp and steady look at the man. "But your partner is. I'm guessing he's the one who shot the convenience store clerk. What's to stop him from burying you right alongside us if it means another half million for himself?"

Deke's face washed bright red then went stark white. "Stop trying to make trouble."

"Trouble?" Rogan lifted his eyebrows. "I call it truth."

"Shut up!" Deke's tone did a fine imitation of his untrustworthy partner's commanding snarl.

Rogan shrugged and turned away, continuing to assess the environment.

"Uh-oh!" He exhaled sharply.

"What?" their captor snapped.

Rogan jerked his chin toward a highway patrol car pulling up to a pump several lines down from their own.

Deke swore. "I gotta warn Barry."

"Too late," said Trina. "He's gone inside to pay."

Their captor swore again, his voice shredding as if his vocal cords had morphed into razor blades. Sheer panic if Rogan had ever heard it. Deke's eyes went wide as dinner plates as first a female patrol officer emerged from the car and then a male officer, who went to the pump. The woman straightened the tool- and weapon-laden belt around her waist as her gaze coolly scanned the area.

Rogan's muscles tensed. Almost showtime.

Then his jaw dropped on an intake of breath as his gaze fastened on the convenience store's front door, which was visible over the female patrol officer's shoulder. A familiar figure walked out, paused, and looked around. Buzz Draper, a grizzled veteran of the road and one of the truckers who hauled contraband for Stathem. Draper's gaze caught and hesitated on the patrol car with the attending officers then fell away as he ducked his head and strode toward a semitruck and trailer parked in the shadows, engine idling, about twenty yards on the opposite side of the pickup from the patrol car. That truck had to be hauling drug contraband.

Rogan swiveled his head from the big rig to the highway bulls' vehicle and back again. He and Trina were sitting with an armed robber in a stolen truck sandwiched between representatives of the law who wanted nothing better than to arrest them and a worker for the cartel that wanted to kill them. The perfect storm that could either spell deliverance or disaster.

EIGHT

What was going on with Rogan? Trina sat up straighter. First he'd let out a pained gasp. Probably that young thug back there did something to hurt him. Then a second gasp. Surprise, not pain. Her hand went to the release on her seat belt. She needed to be ready to move.

Even as she unlatched the belt, Trina turned her head toward a flurry of activity in the back seat. Rogan was twisting the rifle away from Deke. The weapon suddenly discharged and exploded the passenger side window. The blast rang in Trina's ears even as the odor of cordite stung her nostrils. Rogan gained control of the weapon with one hand as he slammed his opposite fist into Deke's chin. The man slumped, eyelids fluttering. Rogan reached into their captor's jacket pocket and came out with the box of shells for the rifle.

"Let's go." He jerked his chin toward the passenger side—away from view of the highway patrol officers who'd suddenly gone rigid at the sound of the gun blast.

Trina scooted over and piled out the damaged door as Rogan hopped out of the rear seat, the Tikka in hand.

"Keep low and follow me," he whispered and crouch-trotted away into the gloom beyond the array of pumps.

Trina imitated his scurry as shouts sounded in the vicinity of the stolen pickup. She didn't look back. Their way free was forward. They seemed to be heading for a semi. While efficiently reloading the rifle, Rogan led them past the rear of the trailer then swiftly up to the passenger side of the tractor.

He ripped open the door and pointed the Tikka at whoever was behind the wheel. "Hiya, Buzz. How about giving us a ride?"

The driver yelped. "S-sure. Hop in, Ryan." The stammer sounded anything but welcoming. But then, who welcomed having a gun in their face?

Rogan disappeared inside, and Trina hoisted herself up behind him. So far, maybe thirty to forty-five seconds had passed since their escape. No doubt the highway patrol officers were only beginning to sort out what had happened. But it wouldn't be long, and they'd be looking for whoever else had been in that pickup.

"Back here." Rogan's voice came from the dark void of the cab behind the driver, who shot a wide-eyed glance at her. "In the sleeping berth. We need to stay out of sight until we're well away. But you," he said, the front end of the rifle appearing and nudging the back of Buzz's head, "need to get this thing in gear and drive. Now! But nice and easy so it doesn't look like anything's wrong."

Without another word, the driver wrestled the truck into gear and headed the big rig for the rear exit of the truck stop.

"Hand me your cell phone and shut off the CB radio," Rogan said to Buzz.

The man scowled, pulled his cell from his shirt pocket and tossed the item toward the back. It whizzed past Trina's head, narrowly missing her nose.

Rogan prodded Buzz in the shoulder with the rifle. "Pull a stunt like that again, and I'll lay the butt of this gun alongside your head. The radio now," he prompted. The driver hurriedly complied. "As soon as I pull the battery from that cell you tossed, you'll officially be off-grid. Heading for Rock Springs, I presume?"

"You know the route." Buzz's tone was sullen.

Trina gripped Rogan's arm. "You're familiar with this guy from your undercover work? He transports drugs like your father did?"

"That's right," Rogan said. "Only Dad did his driving on the East Coast. In the West nowadays, Wyoming is a major drug transportation hub because of the three interstate highways running through lots of wide-open spaces."

"And this guy called you Ryan because that was your undercover name."

"Yeah," the driver said. "But we're not used to calling him by his real name yet. Rotten DEA plant." The last three words were spoken in an angry mumble as he merged the truck onto the I-80.

"New flash, Buzz," Rogan said. "You're under arrest." He swiftly recited the Miranda warning. "And you're not going to make it to Rock Springs. At the Highway 287 exit, head north and then east toward Casper."

"We're returning to Casper?" Trina asked. "What happened to Denver?"

"I'd hoped we could hole up and take some time to heal before going on the offensive, but thanks to Barry and Deke, we've lost our bankroll and the luxury of a mini vacation. As soon as that pair blabs what they know to the cops, who should have them in custody by now, the people who are hunting us are going to notice that we were heading south, so now we want to go north."

"And return to a place our hunters will assume we would avoid like the plague."

"Sharp has got to be your middle name."

Warmth spread through Trina's insides at the compliment paired with Rogan's heart-stealing, lopsided grin.

"I still have questions I need to ask my handler," he said, "and now I can give him Buzz and what I know has be illegal cargo back there as a present to help prove my integrity. Why don't you grab some sleep while I ride herd on our driver?" Rogan patted the rifle.

"Don't be needlessly noble. You're the one who should rest. I'm perfectly capable of keeping Buzz on the straight and narrow."

Rogan let out a brief chuckle. "Capable is your other middle name. All right, but wake me up if something seems off—like anyone following us—or when we get within a half hour of our destination."

"Deal." Trina crawled forward into the passenger seat and then accepted the rifle from Rogan.

A deep sigh and rustles from the shadows in the back told her he was stretching out. She unzipped her jacket, since the semicab was cranking out more than adequate heat, then buckled her seat belt. Settling in, she cradled the Tikka in a position with the business end pointed in the driver's general direction. Buzz shot her a sour look. She awarded him a cold smile. Silence fell.

Trina divided her time between checking the mirrors for headlights that seemed glued to their tail and watching the driver for any moves that seemed off. Road conditions were decent with minimal ice and snow, and traffic was light and grew lighter as they rolled farther and farther into the countryside. No one stayed behind them for very long. The vehicles either passed the semi or turned off. But as Trina observed the driver, an impression gradually grew on her. Buzz couldn't seem to keep his eyes strictly on the road. Something in the glove compartment kept attracting his glances.

With a soft hum, she reached out and undid the latch. The compartment fell open, revealing a nine-millimeter Sig Sauer semiautomatic pistol.

"Nice!" She hefted the weapon. "My gun got taken from me, and somehow I don't think you're going to be needing this one anymore." She tucked the pistol into her waistband.

"Listen to me," the driver hissed. "You shouldn't be with this guy. Sooner or later, he's going down. Just a matter of time. Stathem will be grateful if you turn him over. Probably let you live. Maybe even pay you a reward."

Trina laughed. "I've met your boss face-to-face. He didn't strike me as the forgiving type, and I've caused him plenty of trouble. Besides, cash for crooked dealings may motivate *you*, but the idea turns my stomach."

"Fine for you, Ms. High and Mighty, but don't ever say old Buzz didn't give you a chance to come out of this with a whole skin."

"No worries about that. Old Buzz might make better use of his time thinking about saving his own hide. Once Rogan hands you over, you should consider cutting a deal. Sounds like law enforcement is eager to shut this drug trafficking operation down and might give a lot to gain your information and testimony."

"What are you, a lawyer or something?"

"A veterinarian."

"Then keep the legal advice to yourself. I'm a dead man the minute the cops get me into an interrogation room."

"Because that's the way Stathem works?"

An icy knot suddenly congealed beneath Trina's breastbone. If Buzz figured himself for a goner when he was taken into custody, then Buzz had to be a desperate man. On the heels of the realization, his hand darted out, grabbed the barrel of the Tikka and yanked. The rifle sprang from her grip. The man let out a savage roar as he whipped the hardwood butt toward Trina's head.

* * *

Rogan lunged with all his might and caught the rifle stock a hair's breadth from cracking Trina's skull. Snarling and cursing, Buzz wrestled him for possession of the weapon. The truck swerved out of control. A muzzle flashed in a sharp explosion—not from the rifle. Buzz screamed, releasing the Tikka then grabbing his lower right leg tugging the limb toward himself. With pressure removed from the accelerator, the truck immediately began to slow down, but they were headed for the left-hand ditch. As Rogan secured the rifle, Trina grabbed the steering wheel, but she overcorrected and, tires screeching, the semi and trailer began to jackknife.

"Other way!" Rogan cried out.

Trina turned the wheel gently the opposite direction, and the truck straightened out, continuing to lose speed. Swiftly, Rogan scanned the road ahead then checked the side-view mirror for traffic behind them. Nothing. Not atypical for the middle of nowhere in the dead of the night in Wyoming. Good thing for all concerned.

Somehow, from the passenger seat Trina managed to angle her foot over onto the brake pedal and slow the truck to a coast. But it was a contortionist position that couldn't be held for long, and the strain must hurt her wound terribly.

"Help me move this guy to the rear compartment," she said. "Then I can take his place and put on the brakes to stop us."

Together, they wrestled a moaning Buzz over into

the seat into the sleeping berth. Trina could only spare one hand to help as she kept the other one on the wheel and most of her attention on holding the truck on the road. Nearly forever later, they succeeded in moving Buzz. Trina was able to hop into the driver's seat and bring the semi to a complete halt along the side of the road.

Rogan's pulse beat painfully in his wound, and his breath came in gasps, but at least they weren't laid out sideways in the ditch, a mangled wreck and most likely dead.

"You shot me!" Buzz's voice squealed out a good octave higher than normal.

"How did that happen?" Rogan eyed the man slumped against the wall of the cab.

Her breath ragged, Trina waved a pistol in the air. "I found it…in the glove compartment…shortly before this guy launched his panic attack."

"Okay, yeah. I woke up in time to hear the part about him figuring himself a dead man if he got turned in to the DEA. Must have slept through the moment you found the gun."

Trina gazed back at him over her shoulder, her dark eyes luminous. "Thank you for stopping him from crushing my head."

"My pleasure." Rogan glared at Buzz, who wouldn't meet his gaze.

"I'd better bind up that wound," Trina said. "I'm pretty sure I just put a bullet through the calf, but we should do what we can."

"I'm going to do more than bind up his wound. I

wonder if there's some rope around here to truss him up properly."

"Don't expect me to tell you." Buzz's words spat out like something bitter lay on his tongue.

"No worries." Trina offered Rogan a slightly wobbly smile. "There was a roll of duct tape in the glove compartment where I found the gun."

"Perfect."

Fifteen minutes later, Trina had treated and dressed the flesh wound as best she could, using the rig's small first aid kit. And Rogan had used most of the duct tape turning Buzz into a harmless bundle. The man's foul protests had earned him a strip of tape over the mouth for good measure. They left him in the sleeper compartment. At least as far as his leg wound and immobilized position would allow, he'd be somewhat comfortable. That was more than Rogan could say for himself.

"I'm going to have to drive," he told Trina as he got behind the wheel.

"You sound nervous about that," she said, settling herself on the passenger side.

"I am. I may have spent a lot of time in a semi watching my dad drive, but I didn't even have a learner's permit for a regular vehicle when he got arrested."

Trina snorted. "Are you going to try to convince me that a hard-core trucker never gave his son a few semi-driving lessons off the books?"

"I won't try to convince you of that." A reluctant grin stretched his face. "But the hands-on lessons didn't amount to much. I warn you. I'm going to be worse than a rookie at this."

He held the clutch pedal down and attempted to toggle the proper switches on the shift lever while moving the shifter into a position that gave them forward motion. The gears ground, and he winced, but the truck rolled out, and they were on the road toward Casper once more.

"I'm sorry you didn't get much sleep," Trina said.

Rogan shrugged. "At least I got some. I've learned to do with very little."

"I can't imagine the high stress involved in a career as an undercover agent. Do you want to talk about it? Maybe tell me a little more about what happened in Rock Springs when your cover was blown?"

"You mean, did a civilian actually get shot?"

"Not my question at all. If an innocent was gunned down, I know it wasn't your gun that did it. I *know* it."

Rogan felt more than saw the intensity of her gaze on him. He didn't dare meet her eyes. He'd melt. His heart warmed toward Trina more than was wise, considering they had no future together. Did he want the pleasure of her company indefinitely into the future? Absolutely. Could he think of a feasible way for that to happen? Absolutely not.

How long had it been since someone offered him such raw trust? Even as a DEA agent, some of his coworkers had looked upon him with a degree of mistrust because of his family history. But that very history was why he'd been selected to go undercover in an environment that wasn't totally unfamiliar to him. Now that he was labeled a rogue, those who'd eyed him with suspicion were probably feeling justified. Mistaken opinions shouldn't hurt, but they did.

Rogan cleared his throat of a sudden thickness. "I was one of Trent Stathem's personal bodyguards. His favorite, actually, because a few months ago I spotted and stopped an attempt on his life by a rival cartel that his other bodyguards didn't see coming. As a result, I was tight with him and in a prime position to ferret out the identity of the top boss. I was getting a distinct idea about who it was, but I couldn't prove it yet. It was like I could see the finish line on my assignment—almost touch it. All I needed was a little more time to find that proof, but then Stathem got a phone call that ended my investigation and almost ended me."

"You know who the top boss is?" Trina asked. "Isn't there someone you could tell?"

"I have my suspicions, but without proof, no one I could tell is likely to believe me."

"Who is it?"

"Better if you don't know."

"Cut it out. I'm in too deep for it to matter if you tell me or not."

"All right, but not here and not now." Rogan jerked his head toward the back where the driver lay.

It was okay with him if Buzz knew Rogan was still doing his job for the DEA and blabbed that information to his interrogators, but he drew the line at speaking a name until he knew for sure he was right. Besides, if Buzz told his interrogators at the agency that Rogan had an idea about the big boss's identity, the guy might make a rash move and expose himself. A longshot, but still a shot.

"Fair enough," Trina said. "Finish your story."

Rogan changed gears on the truck and increased speed. He was starting to get the hang of the big rig.

"We were in a cartel warehouse in Rock Springs when the call came," he said. "I was standing right next to Stathem and watched his expression change. He got his death look, and those eyes were fixed on me. He was already going for his gun, so there wasn't going to be an opportunity to bluff. I had to act fast. I grabbed him as a hostage to get me out of there alive and turn him in to the DEA as sort of a consolation prize, but there were too many cartel goons to keep my eyes on *and* maintain control of a brute like Stathem. He got away, and a lot of lead started flying."

Trina shuddered. "Wow! Talk about high intensity. But how did a civilian happen to be in the warehouse?"

"As far as I'm aware," Rogan answered, "no non-cartel members were in the building, so how a supposedly innocent civilian got shot, I have no idea. I got hit trying to reach one of the cartel SUVss, so I went with plan B and grabbed the nearest mode of transportation—a motorcycle belonging to one of my fellow bodyguards. A couple of hours later, I wound up in your barn pretty much bleeding out. Thank you for treating me and saving my life."

"You are absolutely welcome." Trina touched him on the arm. "The phone call that set all that off was from the mole in the DEA?"

"No, I think it was from the shadow boss. There was

always an uncharacteristic slump-shouldered posture about Stathem when he was talking to the top dog. But the only person who could have exposed my identity to the big boss, who then passed the information along to Stathem, was a traitor in the DEA."

"But who could the mole be? You said earlier that you don't think it's your DEA handler."

"Jay's not excluded from my suspect list, but he's not at the top, either. If my handler were the mole, I don't think I would have gotten as close to exposing Stathem's mystery boss as I did. I need to find out from Jay who, other than himself, knew about my undercover status—and especially if someone got looped in recently. And I need to have that conversation privately, face-to-face."

"How are you going to accomplish that without getting yourself arrested?"

"Very carefully, and with this load of cartel drugs as both bait and distraction."

"You need to let me help."

"I'm counting on it, but you also have to understand that I'll never forgive myself if something happens to you." Rogan's throat tightened, constricting his voice.

Could she hear how much she'd come to mean to him in such a short time? This woman was a keeper. Too bad she could never be his to keep. She'd made it clear she didn't want a relationship with a guy in a dangerous occupation. Besides, she'd made a good life for herself in a rural area, but Rogan was looking toward a duty post in a big city. How could their lives possibly mesh? And yet something deep inside him yearned for the impossible to somehow become possible.

"I'll be careful." Her tone was soft, reassuring.

But no one could give assurances. What they were involved in was as dangerous as it got. *God, help us.* His prayer was short, simple…and desperate.

NINE

"What are you doing?" Trina asked Rogan as they stood at the rear of the semi in the vague light of predawn.

Holding the heavy-duty flashlight they'd found in a cubbyhole of the sleeper compartment, she glanced around the area in the heart of Casper's manufacturing district. They were surrounded by drab warehouses and factory buildings. Deserted now in the wee hours. A mournful wind moaned through the tight spaces between the crowded structures, and she hugged herself against the chill despite the protection of her thick jacket.

"Finding the drugs so I can put them on obvious display." Rogan reached up with the bolt cutters from the truck's toolbox and snapped the chain that fastened the double doors of the trailer. "Every shipment contains legitimate cargo with the illicit drugs hidden among or even within it. For instance, a load of bicycles might look totally innocent until you slice through welds, take them apart and find cocaine stuffed into the hollows of the bike frame."

"Clever!"

"One of the reasons this cartel has been operating so long and successfully." He unlatched the door bolt and opened the rear of the semi. "Illuminate what we've got."

She flicked the switch on the flashlight and played the beam over the contents of the trailer. Large crates were stuffed in tight from top to bottom, each one stamped Bathtub in large black letters.

"How does anyone hide drugs in a bathtub, especially if the tub is made of steel or cast iron?"

"I don't expect the contraband to be part of the tubs themselves. It'll be part of the crates. On items of this bulk, who's going to notice a slight thickening of the crate walls or a small variance in weight per container?" Rogan heaved himself up into the rear of the trailer and reached a hand down toward Trina. "Hammer, please."

She passed the item up to him, and he used the claw to pry the end from one of the crates then the flat end to splinter the wood.

He let out a low whistle. "Look."

Trina peered up at the hand he was holding down toward her. His palm held several tiny baggies filled with fine, rosy-gray powder.

"What is it?"

"Heroin."

"From seeing pictures during drug education in school, I thought heroin was white."

"In its purest form it is, but this stuff is cut with additives and packaged ready for the street. Probably would have ended up all over the Southwest if we hadn't diverted it. We're done here." He hopped to the ground and closed the double doors.

"Now we go call the DEA to come and get it and the gift-wrapped driver?" Trina fell into step with Rogan as they strode away from the semi. "Merry Christmas and happy New Year to your friends, all in one grand gesture."

He glanced at her, a frown playing around his mouth. "Friends? Not hardly. Before I entered the field, I made it a point to familiarize myself with the personnel in the Wyoming DEA and to stay current with any changes, but only on paper. I've never met anyone from the Casper office except Jay. Other than him, only the special agent in charge of the post even knew I existed until, all of a sudden, I'm a blown undercover agent gone rogue. They're going to be just as rabid to hunt me down as the cartel."

On impulse, she wrapped her hand around his. His palm was warm and firm, and he closed his fingers around hers. What did it mean that the connection instantly created a sense of belonging, of peace in spite of turmoil?

"I'm sure a great many of them will be glad and relieved when the truth comes out," she said softly. "And not just because a rogue agent is a potential embarrassment to the agency."

"I hope you're right—about them being glad and about the truth coming out."

He smiled at her and Trina's heart expanded almost too big for her chest. If only she could allow herself to fall for this guy. If only she wasn't already mostly there. She dragged her gaze away from his.

"But for now," he continued, "if you've got a few bucks in your handbag, we need to grab a taxi to a twenty-four-hour diner I know. They've got the best pancakes I've ever tasted."

"Pancakes!"

"Yup. Never take down bad guys on an empty stomach."

"Is that some kind of unofficial DEA motto?"

"Nope, that's an original Rogan McNally philosophy. When we're about halfway through our meal, I'll use Buzz's cell phone to call Jay on his home landline. It'll be bugged, of course, on the chance that I'll reach out to him. I'll tell him about the truck, and the agency won't be able to ignore the tip. They'll swarm all over it, but since I'm going to use a keyword in my conversation with Jay, he'll know to meet me at the diner instead. And come alone and quick."

Trina's heart skipped a beat. "But what if he's a crook?"

Rogan shrugged. "If he still believes in me, he'll show solo. If he's honest but thinks *I* might not be, he'll bring backup from the PD, since the field staff from the Casper DEA office will be busy at the truck. And if he's the mole, he'll send in the cartel. Any way it plays out, I'll know where I stand."

They reached a moderately busy city street, and Rogan hailed a cab. Half an hour later they sat in a cracked and well-worn diner booth, gobbling pancakes like it was their last meal. Which it very well might be if someone showed up to shoot them. The negative thought pecked at the back of Trina's mind.

Rogan's phone conversation with his handler had seemed to go as well as could be expected. Of course, the guy urged Rogan to turn himself in, but Rogan deflected by asking how his buddy Ethan with the marshals' service was doing. Apparently, the federal deputy was going to pull through fine. And then the information about the location of the drug-smuggling truck completed the distraction from Rogan's status as a fugitive. If Trina hadn't known there was a keyword somewhere in the conversation, she wouldn't have noticed anything cryptic in what had been said.

"Bingo!" She held up a pointer finger as she swallowed her last bite of fluffy banana-walnut pancakes drizzled with chocolate sauce.

"What?" Across from her in the booth, Rogan narrowed his eyes at her.

"That was the keyword. You answered 'Bingo!' when your handler suggested that the cartel might be creating a smoke screen in saying that you stole a million bucks from them."

"Sorry. Not my word." A slow grin spread across Rogan's face that somehow seemed to thin the air in Trina's lungs and create little flutters in her pulse.

What was up with that reaction? She was long past her teenage years.

"In using the phrase *smoke screen*," Rogan went on, "Jay was letting me know that the situation at the agency is murky right now and the truth hard to discern. My key word for asking him to meet me privately was *check*. When I told him that the agency needed to go check out that truck."

"So, basically, there was a conversation going on within a conversation."

"Pretty much. Now we need to get ready for company. Jay—or Jay and unknown others—should be here sometime in the next ten to fifteen minutes." He scooted out of the booth, and Trina followed suit.

Instead of heading for the front door, Rogan walked through the batwing doors leading into the kitchen. Trina stayed on his heels. None of the three staff members seemed to mind that their space had been invaded by customers. In fact, one of the cooks winked at Rogan, who winked back.

"They like you here," Trina whispered to Rogan as they hustled up a narrow set of back stairs, savory cooking aromas following on their heels.

Rogan grinned over his shoulder at her. "Jay doesn't know the real reason why I like meeting at this diner. Remember I told you I spent three years in foster care with a nice family? Well, Daniel, the head cook—who is also part owner of this establishment—is my foster brother."

"So, you feel safe here?"

At the top of the stairs, Rogan opened a door, and Trina followed him into the living room of a small but neatly kept apartment.

"I know I'm with people I can trust." He took off his jacket and unslung the rifle from his shoulders. "But I hate potentially bringing danger to their doorstep like I might be doing right now. If there were any other place I could go, I'd go there."

"Not hard to understand." Trina did a slow turn, observing the practical, minimalist decor. "No woman's touch. Your foster brother isn't married?"

"Sure, he is—to this diner." Rogan went to one of a pair of windows, rifle in hand.

Trina went to the other window, parted the curtain and peered out. The view was of the street in front of the diner.

"When Jay arrives," Rogan said, "I'll give him a few minutes to get settled downstairs while we watch from here to see if he came alone. If I'm satisfied that he's flying solo, I'll go down and join him."

"But I should stay here?"

"Please. And continue to keep watch. I'll leave the rifle with you but take the handgun with me."

"Sounds like a plan." She handed him the Sig Sauer that had come from Buzz's glove compartment. "How do I alert you if I see suspicious activity outside?"

Rogan motioned toward a side table. "Chances are I'll spot it, too, since I'll make sure to sit by a window, but you can use Daniel's landline to call the cell we took from Buzz. Here's the number." He wrote it down on a pad of paper sitting next to the phone then he turned toward her, his vivid blue gaze burrowing into hers. "Whatever happens, stay put here. Don't betray your presence, even if I get killed or captured. When it's all clear, let my brother help you relocate to a safe place under a different name. If I'm out of the picture,

I don't think Stathem will spend a lot of time and effort looking for you. Just exercise prudence and settle someplace far away from Wyoming and resist the urge to contact old friends."

Trina's face heated. "How can you ask me to sit on the sidelines after all we've been through together? I'm as invested as you are in proving your innocence and bringing the bad guys to justice. And I'm not being all that noble. It's the only way I can get my life back."

"I understand." Rogan reached out and laid a warm hand on her uninjured shoulder. "But sometimes survival means a person has to start a new life."

A new life? Her insides twisted into a knot. Rogan didn't know what he was asking. She'd lost her husband and father to events outside her control. Now she was supposed to tamely let go of her property, her friends, her animals, and her veterinary practice and become someone else?

"Not happening." She crossed her arms. "We go down together or we come through together."

Rogan let out an exasperated noise. "Trina, I need my head fully in the game. I can't do that if I'm worrying about—" His attention swiveled toward the window. "Jay's here."

Trina looked out the window. A balding man in a long coat but no cap was climbing out of a tan Toyota. The man crossed the street and entered the diner. Moderately paced traffic continued up and down the street with no vehicle stopping nearby. None of the pedestrians seemed to be showing any unusual interest in the diner, either.

At last, Rogan gusted a long breath, and Trina released the breath she hadn't notice she was holding.

"I'm going down," he said, handing her the rifle.

"I'll be right here on the lookout."

He awarded her that lopsided grin of his as he shrugged on his jacket, concealing the firearm in his rear waistband. Trina's gaze followed him out the door. How strange that a piece of her seemed to go with him.

Rogan hurried down the stairs, his mind filled with the image of Trina's fiercely beautiful expression as she threw his plan for her safety back in his face. *One in a million* didn't begin to describe this woman. Why did he have to meet her under such terrible circumstances? He'd endangered her and blown up her life—a guilt he couldn't shake. And yet, if he could take back his action of hiding in her barn, meeting her, and all that had followed, would he? This wasn't the time to examine the question.

At the bottom of the stairs, he opened the back door of the diner a crack and peered out. The alley was vacant except for a dumpster and his brother's compact sedan. So far, so good. He donned his stocking cap and then, keeping his head low, he traversed the alley and went around to the front of the diner. It would increase the likelihood of Trina's safety upstairs in Daniel's apartment if any potential observers saw him enter from the outside. No one would have reason to suspect she was already inside.

Spotting the shiny top of Jay's head near the back of the diner, Rogan strode up to the booth and slipped into the seat across from his handler. As per specifications for previous meetings in this spot, Jay sat with his back to the door and left the view of the entrance to Rogan. The man's hands wrapped around a coffee cup, knuckles white, and his thin lips were compressed into a pencil line. No smile. Rogan didn't bother dredging up one of his. The situation didn't warrant pleasantries.

"I didn't do what they say I did," Rogan told his handler.

Jay's nostrils flared. "If I thought so, I wouldn't be here, but you'd better have a sterling explanation for what's going on, including the involvement of a civilian female."

"Stathem took a phone call, and just like that I was blown, wounded and on the run," he said, keeping his voice low. "The civilian female, as you called her, saved my life at the cost of Stathem now having his sights on her. The sudden exposure left me with one conclusion." He leaned across the table toward Jay. "There's a rat in our pantry."

His handler jerked back against his seat. "That's a huge accusation."

"No bigger than what's being leveled at me."

"Were you getting close?"

"To the mastermind behind the Wyoming drug trade? I think so, but I'm not saying more until you tell me who else is in the loop on my undercover status."

Jay rolled his shoulders. "Just the top brass at headquarters in Virginia who groomed you and sent you out here, and the special agent in charge for the state of Wyoming. You know we play these undercover assignments very close. The handful of individuals I mentioned have known for the past three years, so if one of us was going to blow your cover, it would have happened a long time ago."

"My reasoning exactly." Rogan nodded. "Which is why we're having this meeting."

Jay took a gulp of his coffee as if he needed the fortification, then set the mug on the table with a distinct *thunk*. "Up until all this went haywire with you going on the run, nobody in law enforcement knew that there was an undercover in the state. Now we all know. Only the public is still in the dark."

"Yeah, I pretty much gathered that the world at large thinks I'm a menace." Rogan let out a frustrated noise. "Nobody else in the state offices had any idea? Someone who was looped in right before I was blown, or who might have accidentally found out? Rack your brains, man. There's a lot riding on this investigation."

"When isn't there?" Bitterness coated his tone.

Rogan totally got it. This job could be thankless and never-ending. No matter how many arrests were made, as long as there were hooked customers ready to do anything, to pay anything to get their fixes, there would be greedy men and women glad to sell them poison. There was a supply because there was a demand. Rogan accepted that fact, but he didn't have to surrender to it.

"I know you believe in what we're doing as much as I do," he told his handler. "But to enjoy any success, we need to keep our own house clean."

Jay sighed and nodded. "There's one little odd thing I can think of. A few days ago, I caught Bill Bannon from accounting coming out of my office. He said he left some expense vouchers on my desk for signing, which I found when I went in, but I had a vague impression that the stack of files on the corner of my desk had shifted slightly. Didn't think much of it at the time."

"Was my file in the stack?"

"You know it wasn't." Jay snorted. "As per protocol, your whole life has been deleted from public record, including fingerprints and DNA, and a whole new life has been invented for you. The file on your real life and mission is not kept at the agency office. I keep it in my home safe. But that doesn't mean Bannon wasn't snooping."

"Doesn't get us anywhere if what he was snooping at couldn't lead to me."

Rogan's handler hissed in a breath and went pale. "My voice mail."

"What are you talking about?"

"After Bannon dropped by, I saw that I had a voice mail. It was from headquarters out east. Apparently, one of the esteemed senators from the great state of Wyoming has been putting the pressure on them to find out what the DEA is doing about the escalating drug problem in his constituency. The guy from HQ said on the voice mail that he wanted to hear progress ASAP from our deep project."

Rogan frowned. "Deep project? If Bannon was somehow able to listen to your voice mail while he was in your office, it's possible he could surmise an undercover agent from that terminology, but it still doesn't give him my identity."

"I can't offer you a ready answer right now, but I'm going back to the office to do some investigating." Crimson began to creep up Jay's thin neck and onto his cheeks. "If that pencil pusher is in league with the cartel, I'm going to expose him and nail his hide to the wall."

"Glad to hear it." A small bit of tension unwound from Rogan's middle. He had an ally. Someone in his agency believed him—believed *in* him.

"Your turn to spill." Jay jerked his chin at Rogan. "Who's our mastermind?"

"You're not going to like it, and it's thin—based on circumstances that smell off."

"No hard evidence, then." The corners of Jay's mouth drooped. "Tell me anyway."

"What senator is putting pressure on the DEA for an update?"

His handler's jaw dropped. "No way! Not Senator Hadley. He ran his campaign on stamping out the drug trade in his state."

"Yeah, and he was doing a reelection tour through Wyoming last month. Stathem went missing for an hour—without his bodyguards, which included me—on the very day Senator Hadley was in Rock Springs. When Stathem showed up again, he was agitated and short-tempered. Well, more short-tempered than usual. He said the big boss was nervous about security in his outfit, and we were to keep our eyes peeled for anyone acting suspiciously."

His handler showed him a blank face. "You're right. That's thin."

"But that wasn't the first time Stathem went AWOL when the senator was in state. It was just the first time I noticed the connection. As I thought back, there was a pretty clear behavior pattern, and you have to admit the theory fits. Who better to keep tabs on the DEA's activities than the lawmaker who makes a point of riding herd on the agency? This recent pressure from Hadley might have caused someone at HQ to loosen their lips to him about the existence of an undercover operation. I'm not saying my identity would have been mentioned, but it would have been enough of a hint for Hadley to send the mole in the Casper office on an intensive snooping expedition to find out."

Jay grimaced and shook his head. "So, I should call HQ and ask if someone there told Hadley about the undercover operation? Nothing like expecting your handler to commit career suicide."

"More people are going to get hurt if we don't get to the bottom of this thing."

"I hate that you're right." Jay scowled at him. "I'll make that phone call."

"Thank you." Every ounce of hope remaining within him hung on those words.

"I'd order you to turn yourself in, but that would be a death sentence for you at the moment."

"For the same reason, I'm not going to ask you to look after Trina."

"The civilian female?" Jay snorted a laugh. "Under the circumstances, we probably wouldn't do any better at that than the marshals' service. Somehow, you seem to be keeping yourself and her out of harm's way."

"More or less, but she's extremely capable in her own right." Rogan offered a mirthless smile as he rose. "I'll stay in touch."

"You know where to find me," Jay answered, staring with a furrowed brow into the dregs of his coffee.

Rogan headed for the front exit. He'd go around back again to rejoin Trina. He stepped out into the cold, and something hard jabbed into one side of his ribs and then the same on the other side. A pair of beefy men had flanked him. They must have been waiting on either side of the door, and the hard objects were no doubt the ends of their pistols. One of them relieved him of the gun in his back waistband.

"We're going for a little ride, Osborne," the other one whispered harshly in his ear. "Or should I call you McNally? Stathem's got a little business with you before he puts you out of your misery. Walk naturally now. We're pals here."

The pair shoved him toward the crosswalk.

How had he not seen these guys coming? He'd had a good view of the street the entire time he was talking to Jay. The only way to creep to the front door outside of his line of sight was if they'd slipped around through the alley like he had done. That meant they'd passed the back of the diner. Had they gone inside and been upstairs? Was Trina all right? He'd never forgive himself if they'd been hurting her while he was sitting below talking to his handler.

Would Jay see what was happening and attempt to come to his rescue? That was a good recipe for a shootout that could result in multiple casualties. Or was Jay the person who had tipped off Stathem that Rogan was at the diner? Maybe he didn't have an ally after all. Was the whole conversation with his handler, including that story about Bannon from accounting, nothing but Jay the mole pumping him for what he knew before handing him over to the cartel?

At his captors' prodding, Rogan entered the crosswalk. Several people were walking a few feet ahead of them, and he kept his pace as slow as he could in order to keep the goons and their guns as far away from them as possible. Their little trio was moving so tightly together that the guns poking Rogan's side were hidden in the folds of bulky jackets. No one in the area appeared to be wise to what was happening. Probably for the best.

Just as Rogan and his captors stepped up onto the sidewalk on the opposite side of the street, an explosion sounded, and the glass of the streetlight shattered directly above them. Not an explosion. A rifle shot. He recognized the caliber.

Bystanders began screaming and running even as the goons jumped to the side and threw their arms over their heads to fend off flying glass. A shard nipped Rogan's cheek as he dived after one of his captors and wrested the gun from his grip. A shot to the knee put the thug out of commission. Rogan whirled to do likewise to the other one before the guy could plug him, but a second rifle shot sounded, and the cartel goon dropped his gun with a shriek and gripped his leg.

"Rogan!" Trina's familiar voice called from the upstairs window of the diner. "Out back!"

He raced across the street and up the alley. Trina already had Daniel's sedan running and was behind the wheel. Rogan plunged into the passenger seat, and she burned rubber getting them onto the road and tearing away from the scene that would soon be swarming with cops.

"Where to?" she asked. "Are we back on with the Denver hideout idea? Daniel won't be reporting this vehicle stolen, so the cops won't be looking for it. He also gave us some cash." She fished a small wad from the purse at her side and waved it at him.

"I owe my foster brother big-time."

"It's good to have family like that. Whether they're blood or not."

"I can't disagree there. Hopefully, no one will figure out he helped us. I've never told anyone, including the DEA, that I fostered with Daniel. For now, let's head for one of those no-tell motels and get out of sight." He gave her brief directions toward a seedy part of town.

As they headed toward their destination, she awarded him a sidelong glance. "How did it go with your handler?"

"I don't know." Rogan's gut churned. "During the whole conversation, I felt hopeful that we had finally found someone who would work on our side, but then I was ambushed outside the diner."

"And that cast the whole conversation into question, because who told the cartel where you were going to be?"

"Bingo! To use your guess at the secret word. Now, my fear is we may be as much out in the cold as we ever were." Rogan groaned and scrubbed his hand over the growing bristles on his face. The palm came away bloody from the scratch on his cheek. "Trina, I have to be honest with you. I have no idea how we're going to get out of this alive."

TEN

Trina accepted a room key from Rogan as they stood under the shadow of an awning outside the office of a run-down motel.

"We've got adjoining rooms," he told her. "Go ahead and take a shower while I drive up to the Salvation Army store about half a mile away and snag us some fresh clothes."

"As wonderful as that sounds, I'm going to walk to the small pharmacy I saw on the next block. Our bandages are going to need changing, and my teeth are officially growing fur. We need toothbrushes, and I, at least, would like a hairbrush, also."

"Good plan. Bring me a comb."

"Do you want a razor and shaving cream, too?" She resisted the urge to run a fingertip along the short beard that had formed on his chin.

He shook his head. "I'm going to let the facial hair grow. Maybe it'll make me look different from that mug shot they've got out on me. Thank you for your thoughtfulness, though." He cupped the side of her chin with his palm.

A shiver that had nothing to do with the cold ran through Trina. As if she didn't have enough to be scared about, now she could dread the heartache that had to be coming when they went their separate ways. That was, if they survived to reach that parting. She backed up a small step. If Rogan noticed the withdrawal, she couldn't tell by his expression.

"Thanks," he said, warm gaze locked on hers.

"For what?"

"Getting me out of that pickle back there at the diner. You've got this habit of rescuing me. I'd be lying if I said I didn't like it."

Trina allowed herself a small smile. "I think we're pretty even in the saving-each-other department."

A shadow darkened Rogan's gaze, and he opened his mouth, but Trina stepped closer and laid a finger over his lips. "Don't start beating yourself up again for bringing your troubles into my world. I'm tired of that sad song. We've got to move forward."

A muscle in Rogan's jaw twitched, but he shut his mouth and jerked a nod. "Let's go to the stores, get cleaned up and grab some sleep. Maybe then we'll be fit to come up with a workable plan."

She handed him the car keys, and they went their separate ways. Within a few minutes, Trina stepped into the pharmacy, the tinny ring of a bell over the door announcing her arrival. She scanned the shop. Straight ahead, a clerk on a stool behind a counter didn't look up, her dark head bent over her cell screen. The top of a stocking-capped head moved through an aisle to her right. The rest of the person was not visible.

Alert to her surroundings, Trina went left and picked up a pair of travel-size shampoo bottles. Heading up that aisle, she scored a hairbrush and comb. In the next aisle, she grabbed toothbrushes and toothpaste.

The medical supplies must be at the other side of the store, where she'd spotted the customer moving. A telltale *ka-ching* at the sales counter suggested that the person was paying and, hopefully, would soon leave.

"Another shoot-out near downtown today, did you hear?" said a mature male voice. "Couple of known drug dealers got hit, but they don't know who shot them."

Trina's heart let out a soundless cheer. Rogan and she hadn't been identified—at least not to the public. What the authorities might suspect was another matter.

"At least the bullets weren't flyin' in this neighborhood for once," a sour female voice answered. Must be the clerk.

"You got that right," said the man.

Footsteps headed toward the door, and the bell tinkled softly as the customer exited.

Trina pulled her stocking cap lower on her head and went to the other side of the store. Quickly, she snatched up disinfectant, bandages and a small container of nondrowsy pain relievers, then, on a deep, fortifying breath, she went to the sales counter. The clerk was once more fully engaged with her cell phone. Trina kept her head down and said nothing as she laid out her purchases. The clerk rang them up with hardly a glance at the items or her. However, the woman needed both hands to bag the purchases, and when she laid her cell on the counter, the headline of the article the clerk was reading slapped Trina in the face.

DEA Snaps Up Million-Dollar Heroin Shipment in the Heart of Casper

The feds had found the semi Rogan and she had brought in. Had their names been kept out of the story? The photo beneath the caption hinted at the answer. A smiling man in a suit shook hands with another smiling man in a DEA jacket. If that wasn't mutual glad-handing, Trina would eat her hat. Sometimes bureaucrats hogging the limelight was useful, though. It kept her and Rogan's names and faces out of any fresh news story.

Trina hurried out of the store and met Rogan back at the motel. She reported what she'd seen and heard and how the clerk had barely looked up from her phone screen long enough to ring up her purchases. He'd had a similarly anonymous experience at the Salvation Army store.

"Folks in this sort of neighborhood aren't much for poking their noses into other people's business," he said as he handed her a sack of women's clothing. Trina closed the door behind him and, after taking a shower, dressing her wound and donning the Salvation Army clothes, answered the call of her pillow. She woke up an unknown amount of time later with her shoulder itching—a good sign that she was on the mend. She sat up at the edge of the bed and checked the cheap digital clock sitting on the equally cheap side table. Seven hours of sleep. More than she'd thought she'd get. It was now late afternoon. The sun would be going down in an hour or so, which was a good thing. Rogan had wanted the cover of darkness before they left the motel.

A knock sounded on her door, followed by Rogan's voice calling her name. Trina rose and glanced in the mirror over the dresser. She grimaced. Sleeping with her long hair still damp from her shower was a sure way to end up with a fine squirrel's nest adorning her head. Snatching up her brush, she began tugging it through the knots while she opened the door to Rogan.

"Did you sleep?" he said as he walked in and closed the door.

"I did. How about you?"

"For a few hours."

She frowned at him. Fatigue shadows under his eyes were present, but his gaze was bright and alert, almost excited.

"You've been plotting and planning, haven't you?"

He nodded. "I hate to say it, but I think we need to try something desperate."

"Isn't that what we've been doing?"

"No, we've been on the run, playing defense. I want to go on offense."

Trina's stomach fluttered. "What do you have in mind?"

"I have to warn you, we're going after a big fish."

She let out a soft laugh. "You're mixing metaphors. Are we fishing or playing football?"

"Maybe a little of both." He chuckled. "First we have to cast some bait and hope the big fish bites. Then we'll have to fake out the defensive line in order to run in for the score."

"Care to explain?" she asked then winced. "Ouch! This brush is hardly making a dent in these tangles."

"Sit down." He motioned toward the only chair in the room. "I'll work at it while I explain myself."

Trina's breath caught, and she clutched the brush to herself with both hands. She couldn't remember when her mother had brushed her hair, because her mother had died of cancer before Trina was two years old. But when she was little, her father used to brush her hair and tell her stories from their Shoshone heritage. When she was married, Rick used to brush her hair and tell her how beautiful she was. She knew that wasn't strictly true by societal norms, but she was glad she was beautiful to *him*. What would it mean if she let *this* man brush her hair?

Stop being silly, she scolded herself. *It means he's helping you get ready to assist him with his plan. Nothing more.*

Trina forced her tense muscles to relax as she handed him the brush then sat down in the chair. For a big John Wayne–type guy, he was surprisingly gentle with her hair. What were the chances that the explanation about his plan wasn't going to curl it?

Rogan drew the brush slowly downward in fits and starts as the tangles caught the bristles. Trina's hair was thick and sleek and shiny black as a raven's wing.

Something about her demeanor when he asked for the brush had let him know that handling her hair was a great privilege. He intended to respect that impression and do a careful and thorough job.

"You have a wonderful touch with hair," she said. "I'm guessing you must have had a foster sister to go with that brother."

"Sorry. Wrong guess. My foster parents ran a horse stable in Virginia. I did my fair share of mucking out stalls and grooming sweaty horses, but my specialty was manes and tails." He chuckled. I was a typical teenage boy, and I figured out if I wanted to impress the teenage girls who boarded their horses with us, braiding the manes and tails of their mounts did the trick."

"Very sly." She laughed. "Even then you had the knack of figuring out what to do to achieve your objective."

"You make me sound calculating, when the move was more instinctive. I just wanted the girls to stop ignoring me and talk to me."

"I'm sure they started chatting your ear off when you presented them with mounts fit for a queen."

He chuckled. "Sometimes too much chatter, but it beat the snooty silent treatment a few of them gave the common stable hand."

"Some folks seem to have a basic need to feel superior to others. Quite often they're hiding something wicked about themselves."

"Glad you brought that up," Rogan said. "I'm sure you've heard of Senator Charles Hadley."

"Who in Wyoming hasn't heard of Hadley?" Trina sniffed. "He's made sure of that."

"Not your favorite politician, I take it?"

She shrugged. "I know he's got a high popularity rating, but to my way of thinking, he spends too much time campaigning and not enough time legislating."

"Good observation." He worked the tangles out of another section of hair. "Which means he seems to spend more time stumping through his state than actually in Washington, where his voters sent him."

"I hadn't thought about it in quite those terms, but yes, I suppose that's true."

"What if I told you I believe the senator needs to be in state frequently to keep hands-on tabs on his thriving drug-trafficking business?"

"What a hypocrite!" Trina squared her shoulders. "No, I'd say hypocrite was a mild label for him. Hadley practically bases his entire campaign on eliminating the drug trade from Wyoming. Shakespeare's immortal words ring true once again. The senator 'doth protest too much, methinks.'"

"You're not shocked or skeptical?"

"I wish I were. So, if your handler is the mole, he knows that you've guessed the identity of the big boss. And by now Stathem and Hadley are aware of that fact, too."

"Yes," Rogan said. "They will also assume that I've told *you* my suspicions, which increases their need to eliminate us both by about a gazillionfold."

"Which means we'd better hurry up and go on the

offensive like you said while they're still reeling from the news."

"Ah, Trina, a quick study as always."

"What's the plan, then?"

Rogan drew the brush through another stubborn knot of hair. "While you were sleeping, I grabbed a newspaper. Turns out Hadley's in state right now, scheduled to speak at a fund-raiser. I want to lure him to a specific location to personally oversee our elimination."

"Which means *we're* the bait you talked about earlier."

"Only we're not going to be where they're sure we're going to be."

"That's the fake-out you mentioned?"

He won the battle with one tangle and moved on to the next. "You know it. But when they come for us, we're going to get audiovisual of Hadley and Stathem together, incriminating themselves."

"And that's the run for the touchdown." Excitement tinged her tone. The woman was warming to his plan.

"And then we're going to take that recording to my marshals' service buddy and tell him about Jay's betrayal of the DEA, and the dominoes will begin to fall. Hadley, Stathem and my dishonorable handler will get arrested."

Trina laughed. "Now, we're fishing, running a football and playing dominoes at the same time."

"What can I say? We're multitaskers."

She laughed but sobered quickly. "I'm going to pray hard that this plan works."

"Of course. You want to get back to your life."

At his words, she stiffened. "Not just me, Rogan. I want *you* to have a life, too."

He finished pulling the bristles through her now tangle-free hair, came around to the front of her and handed her the brush. She stood up, facing him, and their gazes locked. Her dark eyes pulled him into their depths. His arms ached to wrap around her, but he forced them to remain at his sides.

"You are the least self-centered person I've ever met," he told her through a constricted throat. "You've got a heart as big as Wyoming. Whatever happens, I want you to know that I admire you."

Her gaze fell away from his as her cheeks turned a soft shade of pink. "I've only ever wanted to be the woman of integrity my father raised me to be and to live in ways that honor my fallen husband."

"You succeed more than you realize."

She lifted her face toward him, her eyes shadowed beneath long lashes. His gaze fell to her lips. Would she push him away if he tried to kiss her?

A sudden beeping came from his wristwatch, and she jerked and stepped back with a gasp.

Rogan released the breath he had been holding as he contemplated that kiss. "I set my watch to let me know when it was five minutes to five. I want to catch the early news to see if there's anything more that concerns us."

On reluctant feet, he turned away from her and went for the television remote. What rotten timing for his watch to beep. Then again, it was just as well that kiss never happened. Romance had to stay out of their relationship. She didn't want someone in a dangerous career, and he was devoted to his high-risk job and wanted to make a home where the action was—not a quiet, rural area. Didn't he? Memories of the deeply satisfying times on his foster family's horse farm swept over him. He shook off the nostalgia.

Head in the game, buddy. This was no time for distractions.

Rogan clicked the remote, and the television sprang to life. The opening credits of the newscast were just starting to run. Trina perched on the end of the bed, arms crossed, and Rogan pulled up the chair she'd been sitting in and settled into it, mimicking her posture.

"Our top news story," said the female anchor, "is a press conference that took place at noon today in the lobby of the Casper office of the Drug Enforcement Administration, where the public affairs agent, Dean Lawrence, announced the seizure of over a million dollars' worth of heroin that was being shipped across the state of Wyoming.

Bryan Mercer, Casper's mayor," continued the newscaster, "was on hand at the press conference to congratulate the Wyoming DEA for the major seizure."

The report segued to a recorded clip of the press conference. A portly figure with a full head of fluffy gray hair—Casper's mayor—stood at a podium inside a generically furnished lobby with the large letters *DEA* etched on the wall in the background.

"We're grateful, particularly on this day," Mercer said, "to our local DEA agents, who halted a flood of deadly heroin from reaching the streets, not only in Wyoming, but in the surrounding states."

Next to Mercer stood a tall, lean man with military posture and a soberly dignified expression—Dean Lawrence, special agent for public affairs. Rogan leaned forward as the man stepped to the podium and fixed the camera with a sober gaze.

"Our office is committed to the protection of the public from an infiltration of illegal drugs and the lawless and dangerous behaviors that accompany the trafficking and abuse of drugs, such as the heroin we seized today. The driver of the truck was arrested, and we trust that he will be able to point us in the direction of those who supplied the illicit cargo he was carrying. We also want to thank the anonymous tipster who did his civic duty in reporting the location of the suspicious truck so that our agents could perform the apprehension and seizure."

"Huh?" Rogan sat back as Dean continued his remarks. "I'm surprised he mentioned the tipster."

"Refreshingly honest," Trina said.

Rogan rolled a shoulder. "Disingenuous, more like. Finding us has got to be on top of the agency's priority list right now. I doubt our truck driver, Buzz, is actually talking. He'd be too afraid of the cartel. But I'm sure he's given his tale of woe regarding his pitiful manhandling by us to everyone within the sound of his voice. They have to be aware I'm the anonymous caller."

Trina turned toward him, face brightening. "That's good. Then the public face of the DEA in Wyoming just thanked you personally."

"He's telling me to come in out of the cold." Rogan shook his head. "They're not certain whether or not I've gone rogue. Until they know I'm going to be a credit to them, not a disgrace, they won't be making the public aware of my DEA affiliation. So, to the world's knowledge, I will continue being a wanted cartel member."

Trina scowled. "Bringing in that truck full of heroin should be a big hint that you're not a rogue."

"It'll help my credibility when I'm finally able to go in and make my case, but I doubt anyone but Jay and I are aware that the agency is compromised—and I'm even more certain they have no idea about Senator Hadley. My undercover assignment isn't finished until I expose the mole and the master boss."

"And neither you nor I will be safe until Trent Stathem and his crew are behind bars." Her shoulders slumped. "I get it."

They turned back to the TV. Movement behind the public affairs agent caught Rogan's eye, and his stomach curdled. "What's that guy doing there?" He got up and put his face close to the TV.

"Who?" Trina joined him, peering closely at the screen.

"My handler." Rogan pointed to Jay Reynolds, holding a mug—probably containing coffee—only a few feet to the side and behind Dean.

Jay lifted the mug to his lips as the public affairs liaison concluded his remarks. But the gesture was odd in that the man held his thumb out toward his ear and his pinkie toward his mouth while he sipped.

Trina barked a laugh. "Your handler is telling you to call him."

Rogan backed away from the television, squaring his shoulders. "The guy's got a lot of nerve expecting me to chance making contact with him again when he betrayed me to the cartel. I'll talk to Jay Reynolds when I put the cuffs on him for selling out our agency and nearly getting you and me killed."

An image of Trina lying on the ground, bleeding, flashed before his mind's eye, and nausea gripped him. He couldn't lose Trina. He simply couldn't!

What was the matter with him? He didn't *have* Trina in the first place. Clearly, his concern for this fascinating and courageous woman went way beyond law enforcement's ingrained care for any innocent civilian. He suppressed an inner groan. As if this situation could get any more dangerous. Now his heart was at risk too.

ELEVEN

"Don't be stubborn, Rogan." Trina planted her hands on her hips. "We've jumped to a conclusion about Jay's complicity with the cartel that seems reasonable, but it's still just our interpretation of the circumstances. If we're wrong, and there's help to be had in this situation, we desperately need it."

"Contacting Jay again is a huge risk I don't want to take. I've got more than myself to think about." His gaze went dark, his words fierce.

"I understand your concerns." But did she? The intensity of his gaze on her sent a shockwave through her. Such ferocity seemed excessive. Had she become special to him in a personal way? Or was she reading too much into a facial expression and an inflection? No time to examine emotional issues now.

She stepped closer to Rogan. "I think maybe another reason you were chosen for undercover work is your independence and self-sufficiency. Who can blame you? You were raised that way. But this may be one time to put the I-can-do-it-myself philosophy aside. What can it hurt to hear what he's got to say?"

"I don't like it." Rogan crossed his arms over his chest and stuck out his jaw. Tense seconds passed, then he dropped his arms to his sides and gusted out a breath. "But I'm going to listen to you because you have as much at stake in this mess as I do. Wait here a minute."

He went out the door but was back within thirty seconds with something in his hands.

"A burner phone? What happened to Buzz's cell?"

"I threw it away. Since I used it to call Jay, the agency would have the number, and the moment I put the battery back into it, they would be busy triangulating its location. On the way to the Salvation Army store, I passed a bodega that had burners for sale, so I picked one up. Aside from allowing me to make a call, it gave me the ability to voice record my complete report on my undercover activities, including my suspicions about the identity of the big boss, and upload it to my cloud account. That way if—"

"We don't survive, the report exists," she finished for him.

He eyed her soberly and nodded. "Yes, and I texted access information for the account to my friend in the marshals' service."

"One person we know we can trust."

"Right."

"But how are you going to call your handler? He isn't at home and calling him at the office would be extra risky."

"He's got a phone that he keeps with him just for me. This is a private call now, not for show and tell in handing off a cargo of contraband."

"No secret words?"

"Straight talk. If anyone is listening, they'll get an earful."

"*I'll* be listening. Put it on speaker, would you?" Trina returned to her perch on the end of her bed, and Rogan settled in the chair. She practically held her breath as he punched in numbers and then waited. The ringtone sounded once…twice…three times…four…

"Hello?" The word came out a little breathless and with a slight echo.

"Jay, you rat, you sold me out." Rogan's growl raised the hairs on Trina's arms.

"I didn't, man. Let me tell you what I discovered when I returned to the office after the blowup at the diner. I had the tech guys sweep my car, and a tracking device had been planted on it."

The heat in Rogan's eyes dialed down a notch. "Backs up my story that there's a mole in the agency."

"I believe you about that. The device could have been planted here at the office, but not necessarily."

"What do you mean?"

"I'm standing in the agency parking garage right now, checking out lines of sight. The guard at the gate has a clear view of where I usually park. It would have been difficult to plant the device unseen."

Trina nodded as Rogan caught her gaze. Jay's location explained the echoey sound in the connection.

"I'm about ready to head home," Jay continued. "I

need to verify whether or not someone got into my safe with your file in it."

"How are you going to determine that?"

"Interrogate my dog." The man chuckled softly, but the mirth held a hard edge. "Seriously, though, they'd have to tamper with my security system first and then find my safe and then get it open."

"The job would take a professional."

"For sure, but even the pros can leave a trace of themselves behind. If they did, I'll find it. I'm one angry agent right now."

"I don't blame you."

"Keep your head down, pal. Let me call you back as soon as I have something."

"No, I'll call *you* in an hour or so. I've got some ideas about catching these rodents." Rogan ended the call.

"Feel better now?" Trina asked.

He eyed her with a raised brow. "Yes, about Jay. No, about someone accessing my file at Jay's house. But I shouldn't be surprised. Stathem can get those kinds of jobs done, but I'm thinking that hiring a professional burglar with safe-cracking skills might be more up Hadley's alley. Once the mole at the agency clued them in that there was someone undercover in their outfit, no effort or expense would have been spared to discover the agent's identity."

"No effort or expense is being spared in trying to track us down, either. We keep staying a half step ahead of our pursuers, but that can't last forever."

"That's the main reason we have to be proactive,"

Rogan said. "For one thing, we can't stay here much longer. Both the cartel and law enforcement will be canvassing all the hotels and motels in the city. I paid the motel clerk extra to ring my room if someone came around asking questions, but who knows if the guy will actually follow through." Rogan stood up. "Let's gear up and head out. We can hit a drive-through for supper then go park somewhere to eat it and call Jay back."

At the mention of food, Trina's stomach growled, and her face heated. "I guess I could eat something."

Rogan laughed, and she joined him. The touch of humor eased the tension constricting her chest.

Together, they threw on their coats, Rogan making sure that the rifle was completely hidden under his. Trina tucked the pistol taken from the diner gunman into her purse. Maybe she should get a holster and carry on her body. The gun would be handier that way. A lot had changed since this tough, brave and determined man had come into her life, but not all for the bad.

As they prepared to leave the motel, Trina shot sidelong glances toward her companion. Her attraction toward him had steadily grown over time, much to her chagrin. And yet, how could she regret knowing him? Since meeting Rogan, she'd been in more personal danger than ever, but she'd also felt more alive. The numb places that had overtaken her heart since the deaths in her family were thawing out. The self-pitying thoughts had faded away.

If Rogan and she survived this situation, even when they went their separate ways afterward, she'd always be grateful to him for reviving her spirit. She was going to hang onto the aliveness from now on. Suddenly, living long enough to attend the Christmas Eve candlelight service at her church became a guiding goal.

Rogan went to the window, parted the curtain and peered outside. His sharp intake of breath drew Trina to his side. Dusk was falling, but the view outside the motel office was bathed in a weak yellow glow from a dirty bulb in a pole lamp outside the door. It was enough to show a dark-colored SUV parked outside the office, engine running. A pair of large male figures stepped out of the vehicle. One yawned and stretched then followed his partner toward the door.

Trina's heart rate doubled. "Cartel?"

"I have no doubt."

"Did Jay trace our call somehow and tip them off? Maybe I was wrong about him and he *is* the mole." Her gut churned.

"No, I don't think so. Those guys look entirely too casual to be hot on our trail. This has got to be part of a routine sweep."

Trina frowned. "The office attendant only saw *you* when you checked in, and you had on your stocking cap and your scarf wrapped around the lower part of your face. They're going to be looking for a man and a woman together."

"But the attendant is going to remember that I rented two rooms, which may seem a little odd."

"Do you think they'll come check our rooms? Wait—dumb question. Of course they will."

"We'll have to go out the bathroom window and creep away."

"Why can't we get in the car and leave while they're asking questions in the office?"

Rogan glanced at her. "Do you see Daniel's car in the lot?"

Trina scanned the area. "Come to think of it, I don't."

"Under these conditions, I'd never park in a constricted lot with only one exit. The car is around the corner and up the block at the far end of a convenience store parking lot. Didn't figure anyone would bother it if we didn't leave it there overnight."

Trina punched him his bicep. "Thanks for telling me sooner, Mr. Devious."

"You're welcome." He grinned. "Let's go."

They headed to the bathroom, and Rogan strong-armed the window open. The casement was big enough for them to fit through, one at a time, but they had to remove their jackets and gear. Rogan went first, and Trina handed him their coats, scarves and hats, their weapons, and her purse. Then she wriggled out, shivering until he helped her into her outerwear. The air around them was damp, as if more snow threatened.

Rogan's warm hand closed around hers, and he tugged her toward the end of the alley. Visibility improved dramatically as they neared the street, and movement caught Trina's eye.

"Uh-oh!" She yanked Rogan backward and huddled up against him in the shadows as a police cruiser trolled slowly up the street past them.

"Things are getting way too interesting." Rogan's voice came softly in her ear, his warm breath stirring her hair. "As you pointed out earlier, the people hunting us are looking for a couple. Let's split up and meet at the car. Keep your head down and walk fast but casually. You go first, and I'll keep an eye on you until you turn the corner. Let yourself in and start the engine. I'll be there as soon as I can."

Rogan lifted her hand and pressed the chilly metal of the car keys into her palm. She wrapped her fingers around them. Separating didn't appeal to her, but she understood the logic.

"See you there."

She left the alley and moved at a brisk walk, head down, hands in pockets like someone fending off the cold. Very normal behavior in this weather. She rounded the corner at the end of the block, and the sudden lack of Rogan's watchful eye hit her like a physical force, and her steps slowed as her gaze darted here and there, assessing for threat.

The small sedan sat where Rogan had said. The lights from the convenience store didn't quite reach the parking spot, so Trina was in shadows as she reached the vehicle. Gazing around, , she unlocked the car, slid inside and quickly shut the door after her to kill the overhead light.

Then she waited. Rogan would show up soon.

The passenger-side door suddenly yanked open, and she turned toward it with a welcoming smile on her face. The thug that dropped into the passenger seat returned her grin and pointed a semiautomatic at her.

"Now we wait to welcome your boyfriend," the man said.

* * *

Rogan stepped from behind the tree where he'd taken cover when he saw the cartel goon approach the car. Two strides took him to the vehicle as the man attempted to close the door. He blocked it with his body and pressed his gun barrel to the base of the thug's skull. "Drop the weapon."

"What if I shoot your girlfriend instead?"

"Then you'll be dead. If you *don't* shoot my girlfriend and turn your gun over to her *instead*, then you get to live and carry a message to your boss that he's going to want to hear."

"Stathem doesn't want to hear anything from you except begging for your life."

"I'm not talking about Stathem. I'm talking about the man who pulls his strings."

"I don't know how to get in touch with that guy."

"Stathem does, and he won't dare neglect to pass along my message after you give it to him."

Silence fell. Rogan's pulse throbbed in his ears. The other man lowered his gun and allowed Trina to snatch it from him. Rogan inhaled a deep breath.

"What's the message?" The goon's tone was a sandpaper growl. Wounded pride coloring his mood, no doubt.

"Out of the car first." Rogan motioned with his gun, and the man got out and faced him, hands raised.

Rogan took the guy's place in the passenger seat, keeping his weapon trained on the cartel's hired hand.

"Tell Stathem to tell the big boss that I know who he is. Tell him he's cost me my career with this bogus accusation that I went rogue and stole a million dollars of cartel money. Now, I want to meet with him in person, and he'd better bring ten times that amount."

The thug made a scoffing noise. "The big boss will never agree to meet you, and he sure won't pay you to go away when we're going to kill you soon enough."

Rogan leaned out of the car toward the hired hand. "He'll do what I ask, or I go to the media with what I know. Reporters and bloggers don't need as much proof as the legal system in order to quote me as a reliable source. This could blow up on the internet overnight. He could deny it, even try to sue people, but the damage will be done, and he knows it. Just tell Stathem to tell his boss. I'll be in touch with time and place for the meeting."

He slammed the door and didn't need to say a single word to Trina. She gunned it out of the parking lot in a screech of tires.

"You make a compelling case for Hadley to meet with you," she said as they put distance between themselves and the convenience store parking lot. "Politicians can't risk being tried and convicted in the media. If I were him, I'd take the meeting but make sure you don't leave alive. Problem eliminated and I keep my money."

"I'm counting on that kind of thinking."

"But even with you gone," she continued, "he's not going to let me live, either. He'll be sure I know his identity as well, which I do."

"I know." Rogan sighed. "If this meet and greet fails to trap our quarry, and I get killed, then I want you to follow through with my threat and go to the media. That voice recording I made will be like live ammunition for you, but I'd rather reel this guy in and get him tried in an actual judicial court, not merely the court of public opinion."

Trina's glare at him carried heat. "Don't you think for a minute that I'm going to take a back seat when this plan of yours goes down. We're going to need all hands on deck."

"I think I hear a 'so there' in that speech, but it happens you're right. I'm going to need you." Rogan reached over and took the hand she wasn't using to drive.

She sent him a glance, and his heart clogged his throat. Did he glimpse a type of warmth there that, against his better judgment, he'd started hoping to see? Rogan tamped down the surge of feeling. Not the time. Not the place. With what they faced, there might never be either time or place. If they got through the next twenty-four hours, then he could revisit what his heart was clamoring to tell him. But that was a big *if.*

"Let's grab burgers at a drive-through then find a dark corner to park and call Jay," Rogan said. "He's going to have to help us ditch this car, too, now that it's been identified by the cartel."

Half an hour later, they were scarfing down burgers and fries in a shadowed corner lot of a local park. Rogan washed down the last fry with a swig of soda then pulled out his cell phone.

"Same phone?" She lifted an eyebrow.

He grunted. "If we're going to trust Jay, we're going to trust him."

"Agreed."

He tapped in the number and put the call on speaker. Jay answered on the first ring.

"It's me," Rogan said.

"Glad to hear your voice. The woman okay, too?"

"She's fine," Trina said.

"Ms. Lopez." Jay's tone warmed. "Glad to hear your voice. Sorry you had to get mixed up in this."

"That's what Rogan keeps saying. Ad nauseam. I'm here to see this through."

"We all are," Rogan said as a flake of snow hit their windshield, turned to water and dribbled down the glass. "What's the news?"

"Your file at my home was compromised. I know that because when I checked, I found one of the papers out of order. Someone other than me has looked at it. I'm guessing a third-party contractor of either Stathem or the big boss."

"No argument here," Rogan said. "We'd already decided as much, though I lean toward the latter. Contact with him has already been initiated."

Jay let out a low whistle. "You work fast."

"I hope it's fast enough." More crystalline flakes spattered the windshield. "It's getting way too hot out here for us to last much longer."

"Ironic," Jay said. "The weather service says there's another snowstorm on the way."

"Do you think you can get us a clean vehicle? The one we're in is now known to the cartel."

"How about I pick you up in mine in the north parking lot of the Eastridge Mall. The tracking device that was on it has been turned over to forensics. Who knows? We might actually find some evidence as to who planted it."

"We could use all the evidence we can get," Rogan said. "But hopefully we'll have suspects in custody before the results come back."

"What's the plan?"

"I'll tell you in person when you pick us up."

"Okay. How quickly can we meet?"

Rogan exchanged glances with Trina. "Give us forty-five minutes. Pull in and park in a handicapped spot as near as possible to the northeast corner. We'll come to you."

"You got it."

Rogan gave Trina directions to the mall. Less than thirty minutes later they pulled off Caeda Drive via Landmark Drive into the south lot of Eastridge Mall.

"You're still not certain of Jay?" she asked as he directed her to park the car there.

"I'm as certain of him as I can be under the circumstances. But I'm not certain he's as secure as he thinks he is. Let's go watch the north lot and see if Jay arrives without a tail."

They bundled up and stepped out into the lightly falling snow. Flakes caressed Rogan's cheeks and tickled his nose. He pulled his stocking cap low over his forehead and down over his ears and led the way around the building. Peering in store windows as they passed, it was apparent that the mall was doing brisk business as customers strove to make their purchases before the storm hit. With only ten days before Christmas, shopping was in full swing. Brightly colored strings of lights were hung everywhere, as well as other decorations, inside and out.

They arrived at the northeast corner and took up a position in a shaded alcove. Trina moved in close to him, and he put his arm around her shoulders. Their shared warmth was welcome. The scent of the motel's strawberry shampoo carried to his nostrils. If these past few days held any pleasant memories for him, the best was the privilege of brushing her beautiful hair.

Rogan's gaze continuously scanned the environment. Traffic was heavy on East Second Street, one of Casper's main city roads, and vehicles were continually moving in and out of the lot.

"How are we going to know which car is his?" she asked. "It's too dark to see make, model or color, and the snow is getting heavier."

"There's only one handicapped spot left near this location. Jay will have to take that one…and here he is."

A compact car tucked itself into the spot and halted, but the engine did not turn off, and no one emerged. Trina made a move to step out, but Rogan pulled her back.

"Wait. Watch," he said.

Cars were coming and going all over the lot, but Rogan carefully observed the area around the spot Jay had taken. Seconds after Jay parked, a dark SUV slotted itself into a spot one row over. The engine did not turn off, and no one emerged.

"There!" Trina pointed.

"Good eye." He squeezed her uninjured shoulder.

"What are we going to do?" She gazed up at him.

"I'm going to call 9-1-1 on them."

He pulled out his phone and quickly made a call to anonymously report men with illegal automatic weapons sitting in the mall parking lot. Minutes later, a pair of black-and-white police cars pulled into the lot, lights flashing, and headed toward the spot the SUV was parked. The cartel-member's vehicle immediately backed out and zoomed away from the mall, police units in pursuit.

"That was awesome!" Trina grinned up at Rogan.

He returned her gaze. "Are you ready to begin this operation? It's going to be all or nothing now."

"I'm by your side all the way."

The words shattered some sort of barrier on the inside of Rogan.

On impulse too intense to resist, Rogan pulled Trina close and pressed his lips to hers. The moment of gentle connection was there and then it was gone as he forced himself to back away, turn and take the lead toward Jay's car waiting for them. Whatever she thought of his brazen kiss and whatever took place next, he now treasured another good memory from these dangerous days.

TWELVE

Following in Rogan's wake, Trina pressed her fingertips to her lips, where the sensation of Rogan's sudden kiss lingered. What had he been thinking when he did it? Did the kiss mean he was developing feelings for her? She didn't have time to figure it out.

Trina yanked open the rear passenger door and dived inside. Rogan dived in from the opposite side, and they nearly collided in the middle as they hunched on the floor. Without a word, the driver reversed out of the parking space and then peeled out.

Rogan tapped her on the hand. "We should be able to sit up now."

He did so, and she followed suit. Her gaze fastened on the man behind the wheel, sitting straight and tall—taller than she thought Jay Reynolds had been when she saw him on the television. This guy reminded her more of someone else from that broadcast. The man glanced over his shoulder and smiled, and she knew.

"You're not Rogan's handler. You're the public affairs agent for the Casper office, Dean Lawrence."

Next to her, Rogan hissed in a breath. "Why are *you* here? I'm not ready to come in yet. I have to finish my assignment first."

"I'm aware of that," Lawrence answered. "I knew you'd contact Jay again, so I sat outside his house with a laser microphone and overheard your phone conversation with him. The public affairs agent *must* be kept in the loop if we're going to keep a good face on the agency." The man chuckled. "Then I went inside and—ah—persuaded him that it would be best if he let me take the meeting with the two of you."

Trina's stomach rolled. "If you bring us in, you're signing our death warrants. There's a mole in the Wyoming DEA, and Stathem will be able to get to us."

"I know." The man shrugged. "I'm taking you to him now."

"Taking us to Stathem?" Trina jerked back against her seat.

"You're the mole!" Rogan burst out almost in the same instant.

"This war on drugs is a losing battle," the man said. "I figured that out a long time ago, so if you can't beat 'em, join 'em. I prefer to think of myself as an entrepreneur."

"A rodent's a rodent and a traitor's a traitor." Rogan pulled out his gun and pressed it to the driver's neck. "I'm taking *you* in."

"I don't think so." The man lifted his hand and displayed a small box with his thumb pressed on a button. "This is a dead man's switch. Shoot me, and we all go boom in fireworks more brilliant than any holiday light show."

Trina's mouth went dry. "Th-there's a bomb in this car?"

Lawrence chuckled. "Just a simple pipe bomb, but highly effective. If Rogan pulls the trigger, we'll find out how effective firsthand, but it will be our final discovery."

Rogan let out a low growl. "You're not a suicide bomber."

"I am if it's that or going to prison. Agents don't do well there."

Rogan huffed and looked toward Trina. She met his gaze. If only she read an easy answer in those sky-blue eyes. Some plan. But his wide eyes were as blank as hers must be.

"Place all the firearms up here in the passenger seat," their abductor directed.

Rogan's low groan reached Trina's ears as he relinquished his pistol. Insides churning, Trina pulled out her gun and set it beside Rogan's. The rifle soon joined the pile.

"Now, sit back and buckle up," Lawrence barked. "We have a drive ahead of us, and the snow could make travel interesting."

"Rock Springs?" Rogan asked as his seat belt clicked.

"A little farther. The big boss has a private ski lodge near Jackson."

How ironic. Trina pressed her lips together. They

were headed for a spot only an hour away from where all this began for her—her home ranch.

"We're going to meet Hadley?" Rogan said.

"Impressive." Their captor chuckled. "You do know his name. I was wondering if you were bluffing about figuring that out."

"If I can figure it out, other people can, too."

"Not likely, unless they're a bright undercover agent close to the action like you. However, I've been thinking that Hadley may have outlived his usefulness. Stathem, too. What a coup for our agency to bring them down—provided they take fatal bullets during our meeting and can't flap their lips. Then, my bright undercover agent, we take over the operation. Get rich before we get out and enjoy our lives. What do you say?"

Trina opened her mouth to proclaim an angry defense of Rogan's honesty, but he suddenly gripped her hand and squeezed it hard enough to make her wince. She snapped her jaw shut.

"I'm listening," Rogan said smoothly, "but I can already see a few speed bumps we'll have to handle wisely if we're not going to get caught."

Trina gaped at him. Surely Rogan wasn't seriously plotting with this guy. No, she refused to believe it. Her hand went to her shoulder where her wound had begun throbbing again, probably because every muscle in her body had gone as tense as piano wire.

"For instance?" Lawrence verbally prodded.

"What have you done with Jay? He trusts me. If you haven't killed him, it would be good to let him confirm that I told him about the identity of the big boss. He'll back up my story when Hadley ends up dead alongside Stathem."

Their captor clucked his tongue. "Sorry. It got a little rough when I was persuading Reynolds to let me take his car to meet you at the mall. I had to put a bullet in him. Left him bleeding out on his kitchen floor, another victim of the heinous cartel. You can take his place at the office, though. That way, if HQ tries to send in another undercover agent, you can run him and make sure our secrets get kept."

"Too bad about Jay." Rogan shook his head. "I liked him, but we're getting our bases covered."

Trina sent him a sidelong look. Rogan glared a warning at her, but the corners of his lips twitched. She barely made out the telltale movement in the dimness of the car illuminated by streetlights in fits and starts. But the city lights were growing fewer now as they headed out of Casper on US Highway 26, and the windshield wipers were defending against the moderate snowfall in a faint, steady *thunk-swish.*

"What about her?" Lawrence jerked his head toward Trina.

She crossed her arms over her chest. "What *about* me? I'm not Rogan's hostage, you know. I've gone along on this wild ride willingly, because I want to live. Still do. I think I could be useful in this little plan you're cooking up." As long as Rogan's plan included taking this cockroach down and putting him in a maximum-security roach motel like he deserved.

Lawrence let out a deep humming noise. "I heard how you made fools out of Stathem and his crew."

"She's tougher than a marine and smarter than Google," Rogan inserted.

The words about a marine hit Trina between her eyes, and they watered. To measure up to her dad and her hero husband was a treasured dream. The smarter-than-Google part was silly hyperbole, but their captor's silence seemed to indicate he was considering what to do with her—other than putting a bullet in her head and dumping her in a snowdrift.

"We're going to need a replacement for Stathem," Lawrence said at last. "Someone who can coordinate acquisition and transportation."

"A rural veterinarian living near where the mules are loaded up could come in handy," Rogan said, "both as a cover and as a location."

"Mules?" She blinked toward one man and then the other. "I'm familiar with the slang term that means you load the drugs onto human couriers. Why would that be happening out in the boonies where I live?"

"No, we're talking about actual mules." Rogan shifted his body toward her. "There are times when law enforcement is cracking down on trucks more than usual, especially at state borders, and shipping the drugs on the highway routes becomes too risky and—"

"The cartel packs them across the mountains on real mules," she finished for him.

Rogan chuckled. "See? Smarter than Google."

"Takes longer crossing into California by hoof," said

Lawrence, "but we end up with more product reaching the streets safely."

A bitter tang spread in Trina's mouth. How twisted did one's thinking have to become when a person thought of illegal drugs reaching consumers "safely" as a good thing? Rogan squeezed her hand again, and she looked over at him. She couldn't see his face, but she felt his somber gaze. Now, maybe, she was getting a small taste of the gut-wrenching nature of being undercover. That's what they were both doing right now, wasn't it? Posing undercover?

"Grab some sleep," he told her softly. "Things are going to get interesting when we reach Hadley's winter retreat."

"You can say that again." Lawrence barked a laugh.

Trina closed her eyes and settled back against her seat. Sleep? Not hardly. She, if not Rogan, had slept the day away, and now the night held no drowsiness for her. But rest could be important, as well as quiet mental preparation for the coming action.

And prayer? Definitely. Lots of that.

By her calculations, they should reach Jackson around midnight. Would a new day find Rogan and her alive to see sunrise?

Rogan studied Trina as she pretended to sleep. The tightly curled fist on her lap was a giveaway to the pretense. She'd no doubt been shocked at some of his responses to Lawrence, but she had played along very well. His admiration for this woman continued to grow.

Of course, he'd never actually participated in loading mules with drugs for distribution in California—just heard about it in his position close to Stathem as one of the man's bodyguards. Rogan had never carried through any activity that ended with drugs reaching the streets for distribution. In order to establish credibility with the cartel early in his assignment, any buying and selling that took place involving him had gone one of two ways.

One—he'd made the deal but ensured the participants got busted as soon as he walked away. Or two—he made sure the participants got busted with himself included in the net, but with Jay working it so he later got off on some technicality. Using the latter method, Rogan had developed a credibility-building rap sheet to add to the DEA's invented identity for him that was already full of arrests and a little jail time. All of that would be expunged once he emerged from cover and was reinstated as himself.

Legally, as an undercover agent he was allowed, within limits, to break the law he was attempting to enforce, much like a highway cop was allowed to speed to catch a speeder. Par for the course for undercover work—and if he said that aloud, Trina would be quick to call him out on his golf metaphor.

A grin spread across his face. How he loved her teasing. He sobered. Maybe he should leave off the word *teasing* in that sentence. He pulled up short on that thought and gulped against a lump in his throat. These wayward feelings were putting him on a collision course with heartbreak. But he'd gladly take the pain if it meant Trina survived this mess he'd gotten her into.

God, please help me give Trina her life back—whether I'm a part of it or not.

The heartfelt prayer seemed to ease the knot under his breastbone. Time to keep his head in the game, he told himself, not for the first time.

He narrowed his gaze on Dean Lawrence. The back of the guy's head didn't tell him much except he seemed to stay alert. That military bearing never faded. From what Rogan had read of the man's background, Lawrence had been an army captain at the time of his retirement from the military after putting in his twenty. Then the DEA had scooped him up, and he'd risen quickly to public affairs agent in the Casper office on his way to bigger things. If Lawrence had been lured into lawbreaking only *after* joining the DEA, Rogan would eat his socks. People didn't go off track that suddenly. The guy had to have been crooked in the army, too. Once Lawrence was in custody, Rogan would make sure the man's military career was investigated.

"You mentally counting your money back there?" Lawrence said.

"Something like that. What's the plan when we arrive at the lodge?"

"Simple. We get out, we go in and you shoot Hadley and Stathem."

"Seriously? I know we're talking about going into business together, but you already trust me enough to hand me back my gun?"

"Oh, I'll have *my* gun on *you.* At least until you've

taken care of those two obstacles to our budding business dealings. Then I'll know you're locked in for sure."

"Crafty."

"I didn't get where I am by being careless."

"Right. I take it you still have your thumb on that dead man's switch?"

"Nonsense. The digit would be going numb by now. I tucked the controller into a little pocket that holds the switch down, but I can yank it out of the pocket quick as a blink if you try anything stupid."

Rogan raised his hands. "My papa didn't raise no stupid."

"Good. When I found out who you really were, I studied your history, with special interest in your background with your father, young man. It's one reason I'm offering you this opportunity. Figured you'd be able to see the advantages."

A slow burn ignited in the pit of Rogan's stomach. He'd loved his father, but admiration for the man wasn't part of the equation. Rogan had spent his entire adult life attempting to make it clear to the world that he was *not* like his father. Not everybody seemed to want to understand that.

At least in this case, the assumption that the apple didn't fall far from the tree was working in his favor. If Lawrence didn't believe Rogan was amenable to the crooked path, he and Trina would already be dead rather than riding along to the very meeting he'd wanted with the big boss. How things would play out after they arrived at their destination remained to be seen. But if there was one thing the high-stakes, high-tension job of an undercover agent had taught him, it was to act and react quickly in any situation in order to preserve his life and to achieve his objective. In this case, the objective was seeing the whole basket of rotten apples crushed.

As if sensing his bottled anger, Trina's hand closed around his, and she delivered a gentle squeeze. A smile touched his lips. Someone got him. At last. Another tough thing about the undercover life was the pervasive sense of loneliness. Here at the culmination of his assignment, whether it met with success or failure, he was alone no longer.

Thank You, Jesus.

Time passed slowly in the silence and the gloom. The storm howled around the vehicle, but Lawrence guided the small sedan onward at a steady, sedate pace. As they neared their destination and began to see road signs for the city of Jackson, the weather began to clear, though the roads remained icy and snow packed. Short of town, they came to a turnoff onto a county road. Lawrence took the turn and, for about a mile, followed a single-lane path that had recently been plowed. Obviously, they were expected at the A-frame, chalet-style cabin that came into view on the left. Their driver guided the vehicle up the cleared driveway toward the lights glowing warmly through the chalet's windows. He brought the car to a halt next to a pickup truck with a plow blade attached to the front.

Lawrence turned and grinned at them. "We're here, kids. Let's go in and have some fun."

"When do I get my pistol?" Rogan asked.

"As soon as I get the drop on them," their abductor answered.

"How about one for me?" Trina lifted a hand.

"How about keeping your head down in case lead starts flying?" Lawrence chuckled.

"I'm glad this is such a humorous situation for you, Mr. Public Affairs Agent." Trina's tone dripped acid.

The man scowled. "How about I add keeping your mouth shut to that directive."

Rogan ground his teeth together, straining to follow that advice when he'd as soon bite the man's head off for disrespecting Trina. Now was not the time to stir the pot more. Over the last few years, he'd gotten good at waiting for the right moment to make his move. He had to do that now.

Lawrence lifted his arm and showed them the detonator in its safety pocket, then he tucked the device into his coat. Hefting one of the pistols from the pile of weapons on the front seat, he opened his car door and motioned with the gun for them to get out. Brisk winter air nipped at Rogan's cheeks as he stepped into the open.

"After you." Lawrence waved them ahead of him onto the porch.

Trina came up beside Rogan and climbed the steps in tandem with him. A sidelong look at her found what he'd expected—sharp eyes and a determined set to her jaw.

"Go on in, Ms. Lopez," Lawrence said as they arrived at the door.

Trina opened the door, and Rogan followed her inside, their captor close at their heels. They stood in a small foyer that opened into a large great room where a pair of men lounged in easy chairs near a crackling fire—oak wood, judging by the mild but pleasant odor that enveloped them along with the welcome warmth. Lawrence nudged Rogan forward with the pistol in his back and shoved Trina with his hand. They stepped together into the spacious room.

One man rose from his seat, gaze riveted on them. Stathem's sharklike grin beneath the hard, black pebbles of his eyes shot slivers of ice to Rogan's core. There was nothing keeping Lawrence from simply handing Trina and him over to the man's merciless vengeance and, with them out of the way, proceeding with the current operation. Nothing except the crooked agent's ambition, that was. Rogan was counting on that.

The other man rose. Senator Charles Hadley crossed his arms over his chest and focused over Rogan's shoulder on Lawrence. Hadley was no more than medium height and a little doughy around the middle. Not an impressive figure until one came to his finely crafted face and those gray eyes famous for their depth of sincerity, as if he knew and sympathized with everything his constituents were feeling. Not a trace of that trademark empathy appeared in his expression at this moment. The flared nostrils and raised chin spoke of bravado rather than leadership. More was going on here than met the eye.

Hadley's arms dropped to his sides, and he glared at Lawrence. "What is going on here, Dean? You call me demanding I go to my ski retreat in the middle of a snowstorm, and who do I find on the premises but Trent Stathem? I thought you said he and I were not to meet again, that the undercover agent—" he waved toward Rogan "—was getting too close. And now here we all are in the same room. I don't like this."

The bottom dropped out of Rogan's hopes pinned on their captor's ambition. Hadley's weak protests had revealed a wealth of information. The senator was involved, but he wasn't the big boss. Lawrence was and always had been. He was also the king-size mole at the agency.

Rogan turned a hard gaze toward the man who was technically his superior at the DEA. The man shrugged as if the revelation was no major thing. He opened his long coat and drew his sidearm from its holster.

"Hold on just a minute," Stathem cried out. "I want to be the one to put a bullet in this guy. His trouble-making girlfriend, too."

"No, Trent." Lawrence trained his gun on Stathem. "You're going to toss your weapon away."

The drug underboss's jaw dropped, and he froze with his pistol half-drawn in his eagerness to take out the pair who had caused him so much grief. "What are you talking about?"

"We have to make this look just right. Do it... Now!"

Sputtering curses and protests, Stathem complied.

Smiling, Lawrence turned toward Rogan and held out the pistol that had been confiscated from him earlier in the evening. "Nothing changes the plan. Shoot them."

Rogan snatched the gun, but he had no intention of

gunning down the unarmed men, as much as they deserved much worse. Yet, even as he trained his weapon on Lawrence, the man stepped behind Trina, wrapped an arm around her throat and put his pistol barrel to her head.

THIRTEEN

The cold metal against her scalp sent shivers down Trina's spine. Would the next second bring her end? Had she and Rogan come this far to suddenly fail? Please God, no!

"I said shoot them." Lawrence's tone punctuated each word like an ice pick.

"You're only going to kill us all anyway, so why should I shoot anyone?" Rogan's gun swiveled between their captor and Trent Stathem.

The latter had gone bright red in the face. If it were physically possible, Trina wouldn't be surprised to see him burst into flames.

"Yes, why?" Stathem's voice was a snarl. "Why do you want me and Hadley dead? We've been loyal."

The senator stood silent and hunch-shouldered, as if he'd like to fold in on himself. His gaze darted like a nervous rabbit from one person to another.

Lawrence's arm tightened around Trina's neck, and she struggled to breathe.

"Stathem, you and Hadley are compromised," he

said. "I can't have you around anymore. And, McNally, about you I wasn't sure. We could have gone on to do great things together. Make piles of money and live the good life, but no. This was your test, and you failed. Daddy's straight arrow little boy." The final sentence was spoken in a sneer.

Heat blossomed in Trina's middle. "You're disgusting," she croaked out. "A man so twisted you have no respect for hard-won integrity."

Rogan's gaze met hers. His expression was tender, but he shook his head ever so slightly, warning her against further protests.

A swift movement to one side drew her attention. Stathem was diving for the gun he'd tossed away. Lawrence's gun muzzle left her temple and veered toward the cartel underboss. The shot exploded, and Trina seized the opportunity to become dead weight in her captor's arms. Lawrence grunted and lost his hold on her as he sent another bullet toward Stathem. Then Rogan fired a shot, and Lawrence staggered backward.

Charles Hadley's high-pitched screams compounded the din. As Trina hit the floor and rolled away from the gunfight, she glimpsed the senator taking cover behind one of the easy chairs. Not much protection in those, but he curled up into a ball on the floor with his hands over his ears.

Trina came to her knees in a crouch, gaze scanning the violent tableau. Lawrence was nowhere to be seen, but a trail of blood droplets led toward the open doorway of another room in the house. Stathem was down but not dead. Despite blood spreading on his chest, he was lifting his gun toward Rogan—the last man standing. Rogan fired, and Stathem screamed as the gun flew from his hand.

Face white and sinews standing out in his neck, Rogan whirled toward Trina. “Are you all right?”

“I’m fine, Rogan. Thank you.”

“I’ve got to hunt down Lawrence,” he said. “See to Stathem, will you? And watch Hadley.”

“On it.” She scrambled toward the wounded man as Rogan strode from the room, following the big boss’s blood trail.

Hadley remained behind the chair, making small sobbing noises. Trina kept an eye on him as she ripped open Stathem’s shirt. The man lay still on the floor, his dark, reptilian gaze fixed on her. Trina’s skin crawled, but she was committed to the healing profession, and if she could help the creep, she would. He had two serious gunshot wounds to the chest that were beyond her skill without equipment and doubtful even fully equipped. The best she could do was try to stanch the bleeding.

Trina snatched a small throw pillow from the nearby easy chair and pressed it against the close-set wounds, one inflicted by Lawrence and the other by Rogan. Stathem groaned and went limp, passed out. The man’s breathing was shallow and uneven, and a trickle of blood left the corner of his mouth. Not good signs.

Shouts and gunshots sounded somewhere deeper in the house. Trina jerked and turned her head in the direction of the noises. A door slammed, and silence fell once more. She whispered a prayer for Rogan’s safety then returned her attention to her patient. Stathem had stopped breathing. Trina released the pressure on the wounds. The man was gone.

"Hadley?" Her gaze scanned the room, and her heart fell into her toes. That man was gone, too, along with the gun Rogan had shot out of Stathem's hand. She'd allowed herself to become distracted by the wounded man and with what might be going on between Rogan and the rogue agent.

Trina needed to arm herself and go on the hunt for Hadley. She couldn't have him sneaking up on Rogan or escaping now that the net was drawing closed. The rifle and the other pistol were in the front seat of Jay's car that Lawrence had stolen. Trina hurried to the front door and peered outside. The only movement seemed to be the wind stirring the branches in the surrounding woods. In a crouching scurry, she made it to the car and retrieved the weapons. Another quick glance around showed no activity in the yard.

What had happened between Rogan and Lawrence? And where had Hadley gone?

The yard light illuminated a detached two-car garage beyond the chalet. If she were Hadley, she'd be going for an escape vehicle right now. Readying the rifle in one hand and the pistol in the other, Trina headed for the garage. As she stepped under the eaves of the garage roof, running feet sounded from the direction of the house. She whirled, tucking the pistol in her rear waistband and bringing the rifle up to shooting position against her shoulder in one fluid motion. The man—Lawrence, from the flapping of his long coat—was already diving into Jay's car. Trina sent a bullet into one of the tires just as a second figure lunged out the front door at the top of the steps. Rogan, not Hadley, judging by the height of the person.

Rogan fired the pistol in his hand, and the car window shattered at the same moment the engine fired up. The sedan plunged forward, heedless of the blown tire, and geysers of snow spurted from beneath the spinning wheels. Trina's chest tightened. Dean Lawrence was getting away.

Flashing lights suddenly popped into view from the tree line, and a siren blared a brief warning. Two more official vehicles followed behind the first one, firing up their bubble lights. Trina blinked against the brightness, as if the aurora borealis had lit up the clearing around the home. The sedan skidded to a halt then suddenly exploded in a shower of metal and glass. The blast knocked Trina onto her backside. Good thing, too, as a shard of metal buried itself in the side of the garage right where she'd been standing.

"Rogan." The name whispered from her lips as the shooter on the steps stood up from a crouch, dropped his weapon and raised his hands.

Multiple law enforcement personnel leaped, guns drawn, from the three vehicles that clogged the yard in front of the burning sedan. Several of them ran toward the wreckage.

"McNally!" hollered another one who stepped toward the house. "You okay? I'm Ned Stinson from the Casper office. Jay sent us."

"I'm fine, Stinson," Rogan answered. "Trent Stathem's dead, and the guy in the car was Dean Lawrence."

The sound of the familiar voice unraveled all kinds of knots from Trina's insides. Rogan was all right. Her heart leaped and danced. And Jay was alive? Good things were happening. Finally.

"We need to find Trina," Rogan went on.

She took a step forward, her mouth opening to call out, but a hand grabbed her jacket at the same time as something hard jabbed her in the ribs.

"Not a sound," Hadley's voice hissed in her ear. "You're my getaway ticket."

Rogan trod down the steps toward Special Agent Stinson, who was striding in his direction. A great weariness flooded through his bones even as his gut remained tense as a bow string. Where was Trina? She hadn't been in the great room when he'd dashed through it in pursuit of that slippery Lawrence, who'd had the advantage of knowing the house better than he did. Rogan's gaze scanned the yard, but the flickering shadows from the bubble lights and the dying flames from the car played tricks with his eyes.

Stinson stopped in front of him and held out his hand. Rogan shook it.

The guy grinned at him. "Quite the job you pulled off. Jay told us you're legit undercover tasked with exposing the identity of the kingpin behind the drug traffic in Wyoming. He said you suspected there was a mole in the Casper DEA office, but we nearly flipped our lids when Jay told us who shot him." The man sobered. "The agency's going to get a black eye over this.

I'm still processing that I was working elbow to elbow with a crook."

"Jay survived, then? Lawrence thought he'd left him for dead."

"Yeah, well, Jay said the guy should have done a better job of making sure he was a goner. He's hurt bad but should pull through."

"How did Jay know where to send you to find us?"

"Overheard Lawrence on the phone with someone as the guy was walking out of his house. Said something about a meeting at Senator Hadley's cabin."

A lump growing in his chest, Rogan continued to scan the surroundings. "Hadley was here, but he's in the wind. And we need to find Trina."

"Trina Lopez, the civilian female?"

On the heels of Stinson's question, an engine roared to life from the vicinity of the garage. Rogan whirled and began running in that direction, the other agent at his heels. Not a car or truck engine. No, this sound held a familiar buzz-saw whine, and the noise wasn't coming from inside the garage.

Rogan reached the back of the building as a snowmobile took off toward the woods with two passengers on board. One of them was Trina. The other was Hadley, sitting behind her, and no doubt holding her at gunpoint. Rogan raised his weapon but then lowered it. He didn't dare fire, especially in such poor visibility. He'd be as likely to hit Trina as the man who had abducted her. In all the things they'd been through, he'd never known such desperation.

"I'll get a BOLO out on Hadley," Stinson said, lifting a phone toward his mouth. "With a caution about a hostage."

"You do that," Rogan answered, striding toward a large object hidden under a tarp. He ripped off the plastic to expose a second snowmobile, big but old and battered-looking. For sure, no automatic start on this one. "I'm going after them."

"Without a key?" Stinson protested but then broke off as someone answered the phone at the other end of his BOLO call. The man stepped away, barking orders.

Rogan turned on the flashlight feature of his phone and found the latches that held the hood down over the snowmobile's inner workings. Then he reached in and unplugged the set of wires from the ignition switch. He hurried around to the other side of the snowmobile and gave the kill switch a hearty yank. The engine sputtered and spat then died. Rogan set his jaw. This thing had to start. It *had* to.

He yanked the kill switch again, and the engine fired up—a bit anemically, but it was running. With the gauges now lit, Rogan checked the fuel level. Half a tank. Possibly old gasoline, but old was better than none.

Everything in him wanted to take off like a rocket, but that was a recipe for stalling out before he started. He hopped onto the cracked seat, adjusted the throttle, flicked on the headlights and gave the machine a gentle go-ahead onto the path clearly marked by the skis on Hadley's machine.

"I'm coming, Trina," he muttered as he urged the chugging snowmobile faster.

* * *

The cold air bit at Trina's unprotected head and face as she guided the snowmobile between trees and around brush at the insistence of Hadley's gun pointed at her spine. The machine's windshield offered only a modicum of protection from the wind and the occasional low-hanging tree branch. If she got out of this new predicament, she was going to look like someone had beaten her with a stick, which was pretty much the truth.

"Faster!" Hadley barked in her ear.

"Not unless you want to crash," she snarled back.

"Someone is pursuing us."

Trina held her breath and, sure enough, faintly to the rear she caught the sound of a second engine. Rogan. Of that she had no doubt. But how to help him catch up to them without catching a bullet for her troubles? That was the question.

Rogan leaned low behind his windshield, like a jockey urging his mount faster. Now that the engine had stopped spluttering, the old workhorse surged forward. Was that the buzz of another engine reaching his ears over the din of his own? Yes! He was closing the distance, but that also meant Hadley was going to be able to hear his pursuer, too. It wasn't unlikely that the senator had a newer, faster model and would force Trina to increase their speed to treacherous levels in the woods at night. He needed to overtake them quickly while he could.

Gritting his teeth, Rogan pushed his machine to

its limit over the new snow. Fresh powder stung his face, kicked up by the skis, and low-hanging branches slapped his body, but he hung on. Eternal minutes passed. Sometimes he'd lose the sound of the engine ahead and then he'd find it again, as if the machine he pursued was sometimes slowing and sometimes speeding up.

Finding opportunities to help Rogan catch them would be typical of her. The crooked senator may have bitten off more than he could chew by snatching a woman of Trina Lopez's caliber. Yet a merciless fist gripped Rogan's heart. He needed to catch up with her and her abductor, but what would happen when he did? Hadley was a coward, and there was nothing more dangerous and unpredictable than a cornered coward.

Trina held back a whoop that wanted to spring from her chest when they burst from the tree line into a large meadow. Then her spirits dipped again as Hadley renewed his demands that she run full throttle. She'd been able to slow down occasionally in the forest lest they ram into a tree trunk or a downed log. Now, there were no obstacles...except small clumps of rocks that had to be dodged.

Halfway across the meadow, the buzz of the trailing snowmobile increased in volume. Rogan must be in the clearing behind them, but Trina didn't dare look back or they'd hit a rock pile for sure.

Hadley jabbed his pistol into her side. "Faster, or I'll shoot you. I really will."

If the man were frothing at the mouth, he could

hardly sound more rabid. Trina gave the snowmobile a little more juice.

The gun suddenly left her bruised ribs, and she felt more than saw Hadley turn to look behind them. He got off a shot, the blast ringing in her ears. Rogan! If only she could wrench the gun from Hadley's outstretched arm, but she had to dodge a pile of rocks. Her breath stalled when the pursuing engine grow louder and closer, which put Rogan at more risk of being hit. She had to stop the senator from getting off another shot.

Another pile of rocks loomed ahead. Trina aimed the snowmobile right for it. At the last moment, she leaped from the seat, their speed flinging her off hard and fast. She splatted into the fresh powder, plunged right through it and slammed into the frozen layer beneath. The side of her head connected with something hard, and the world went away.

Rogan cried out Trina's name as she flew through the air and hit the ground. The snowmobile with Hadley on it plowed into a cluster of rocks and went airborne, flinging his body like he'd been bucked off a bronco.

Rogan brought his machine to a sliding stop and jumped off it. Every instinct pulled him to run to Trina, who was lying inert in the snow, but he had to ensure that Hadley was disarmed and secure before he could safely tend to her. He found the senator in a huddled lump in a snowbank. The man was alive, but one of his legs splayed out at an awkward angle. Hadley cursed at Rogan as he stripped the gun from his cold-stiffened fingers, unwound the scarf from his own neck and then bound the senator's hands behind his back.

Without a word, Rogan turned and raced to where he'd seen Trina land. She lay still, facedown and half covered by snow. As he drew nearer, the headlights from his snowmobile illuminated a small pool of blood mingling with the darkness of her hair.

"Trina, don't leave me!" The cry ripped from his throat as he knelt beside her still figure.

With frantic hands, he dug the snow away from her head and touched the side of her neck. Beneath the pads of his fingers beat a strong, clear pulse. A soft moan came from Trina, and she stirred.

"Lie still," he told her. "I'll call for help. They'll send a chopper."

Trina lifted her head and spat snow from her mouth. "I'm not lying here with my face in the snow." She rolled over and sat up. Blood trickled from her temple, down to her chin and then off the end of it. She grabbed up a fistful of snow and held it to the injury. "You know head wounds. They always bleed like a person's about to die, but I'm not." She grabbed his jacket and pulled his face close to hers. "I'm not going to leave you, I promise."

Rogan gazed into her luminous dark eyes and drank in the wonder of her cleanly crafted features. Whatever lay ahead for the two of them, he was seizing this moment. He gathered her into his arms and lowered his lips to hers. Trina's eager response turned his heart inside out and drove away every vestige of winter cold.

FOURTEEN

Trina gingerly lowered herself onto one of the old-fashioned but beloved pews in her home church in Pinedale. A soft and lovely rendition of "Silent Night" flowed around her from the piano at the front of the sanctuary, soothing her thoughts. It was Christmas Eve, and Trina was keeping her promise to herself to revitalize her relationship with God regardless of what life dished out.

Over a week had passed since that fateful night at Senator Hadley's cabin in the woods near Jackson. Trina had spent a night in the hospital there, under observation for her head injury. The rest of her had been covered in bruises and contusions that only time could remedy, but her shoulder wound had been deemed healing nicely. However, she was still quite tender in a lot of places, not least of all her heart.

Rogan had disappeared from her life as abruptly and completely as he had come into it. Sure, she'd known he'd be kept close for a while by his agency for debriefing, but couldn't he at least have called her? She was left with the conclusion that he didn't want to call.

In the wake of the arrests of Senator Charles Hadley and DEA accountant Bill Bannon, as well as the deaths of DEA public affairs agent Dean Lawrence—aka the cartel's big boss—and Trent Stathem, Rogan was no doubt busy. Probably enjoying his just reward of picking out his new posting in a big city where the action could be found.

Trina's throat thickened, and she blinked back the tears that seemed to creep up on her at inconvenient moments—like now. Given Rogan's life goals, perhaps a clean break was best for her. For both of them. If only her heart would agree, but it kept stubbornly revisiting that beyond-magnificent kiss they'd shared in the snow.

Even as the thought crossed her mind, Trina's lips tingled. The memory was going to take a long time to fade. She inhaled a long, deep breath, laden with the pleasing scent of pine from the garland festooning the altar. Letting the air out slowly, she closed her eyes to absorb the balm of music written to celebrate Christ's birth, the only thing she should be thinking about on this holy night. As if on cue, the pianist segued into "O Holy Night."

"Is this seat taken?"

At the familiar voice, Trina's eyelids popped open. Slowly, she lifted her gaze to look into the sky-blue eyes she'd begun to think she'd never see again.

"N-no." What was the matter with her? She never got nervous, spoke half an octave too high and stammered.

Rogan smiled down at her, but his grin had a wobble on the corners as if he were no more sure of himself than she was. He suddenly sobered and slid onto the pew beside her.

"Sweet little church," he whispered.

"The people are sweet, too."

"If they're anything like your friends Amy and Jim, they've got to be—but tough and brave also."

"For the most part, though we have all sorts, like any place. But this town does tend to produce salt of the earth. We thrive because we help each other."

"I like that. A lot."

The response seemed more heartfelt than warranted by casual conversation, but she couldn't ask him any questions, because the pastor stepped up to the front and the Christmas Eve candlelight service began. How bittersweet to sing with Rogan, to praise and to pray, and when the candles were passed out and the lights went down, to receive from him the flame of God's love brought to earth as Jesus Christ.

Why was Rogan here? Did she dare entertain the slightest hope that he would stick around?

The glow from dozens of small candles filling the sanctuary ministered warmth to her heart and a fresh peace. She would hurt if—no, when—he left again, but she would survive and do some of that thriving that she'd mentioned to Rogan. Oh yes, she *did* want him to stay, but only if that's what *he* wanted, too.

The service closed with the singing of "Silent Night," and the people gathered in the fellowship hall for hot cider and Christmas treats. Trina squirmed inside. If only everyone would disappear, and she could ask him why he suddenly showed up again in her life. But Rogan's presence at her side drew quite a lot of attention, and Trina had to stuff down her impatience in order to make many introductions. Rogan probably felt like his hand was being shaken off.

Amy and Jim threw in hugs, with Jim giving Rogan's back quite a pounding. Then the pair drew them to seats at a table with them, where they were treated like a pair of celebrities with curious folks bringing them cider and baked goods from every direction and chatting them up. Trina managed a polite façade even as her insides churned, and she stole glances at the man who had stolen her heart.

Rogan leaned over toward her ear. "Not enjoying the goodies?"

Trina grimaced. What should she tell him? She was going to pop if she didn't get to talk to him privately soon? But there was no way she was admitting that. Maybe the standard diet excuse would work.

She forced a smile at him. "I'm going to expand like a balloon if I eat everything on my plate."

He chuckled. "No worries. I can probably eat all of mine and yours, too. Delicious Christmas goodies—especially the homemade kind—didn't feature largely in my upbringing or when I was undercover."

Rogan was acting so nonchalant with her that his arrival tonight must be nothing more than a fond farewell. She needed to brace herself.

"So you're making up for lost time?"

"Something like that," he said. His gaze grew tender as he looked into her eyes.

Heat crept up Trina's neck, and her heart did a little skip. Just when she'd nearly talked herself down to earth, there she went hoping again.

"Can we go someplace private and talk?" he asked.

Finally! She nearly blurted out the word but bit her tongue in time to stop it.

"Sure." The word left her lips a little higher pitched than her normal tone. She gulped back a lump growing in her throat. Here it came. The goodbye speech. Better get it over with. "I'm sure one of the Sunday school classrooms will be vacant."

Trina rose and led the way out of the fellowship hall, though progress was aggravatingly slow with many people calling greetings and stopping them to offer more handshakes and thanks for making a big dent in the Wyoming drug trade. Rogan grinned and handled the attention graciously, but Trina dragged along, her heart bumping across the carpet every step of the way. At last they reached the peace and quiet of a cozy room that served for committee meetings and adult Bible studies.

She took a seat, and Rogan took one beside her. They turned their chairs to face each other.

"How are you doing?" he asked.

"I'm good." She held her gaze on his face, memorizing every plane and angle. If he could be civil and calm, she could be too. If it killed her. "I'm healing fine," she went on. "No side effects from the knock on the noggin."

"Was everything all right at your place when you returned?"

"Better than all right." Trina managed a slight smile at the memory of her homecoming. "The community had cleaned up the yard and repaired the damage to my house, and Amy and Jim took terrific care of my livestock. They got their limo back safe and sound, by the way. And when I walked in the Millers' front door to claim my dog from them, Chica about turned herself inside out greeting me. Best of all, I found out that Stathem told the truth about our county sheriff and the snowplow driver. They really were just knocked unconscious and tied up in the plow garage. They're both doing fine now."

"I'm so glad." Rogan clasped one of her hands in both of his own.

In defense of her raw emotions, Trina slipped her hand gently from his grip. Something dimmed in his eyes. He dropped his gaze and cleared his throat.

"I have some good news, too. Remember the civilian woman who was injured during my shootout with Stathem and his men in Rock Springs?"

"She's going to live?"

"Yes, she is, but she may wish she wasn't. She's facing serious charges herself in connection with cartel activities. We rounded up quite a few of Stathem's crew as part of our mop-up of this operation, and they told us the woman wasn't exactly innocent. She was the cartel's lawyer and was on the premises when the gunfight broke out. Stathem was so angry right after

I got away that he shot her in cold blood because she protested against him hunting down a DEA agent."

Trina pressed a hand to her cheek. "What a relief for you to know that she didn't catch a stray bullet from your gun."

"It was a big relief. And now to get to the reason why I've showed up at your church out of the blue." He smiled and opened his mouth as if he would continue.

"How have *you* been?" she asked quickly. Anything to stall the inevitable farewell.

"Pretty much a wreck." His gaze went somber. "My assignment is over just like that, which I'm glad about and thankful for how it turned out. But you have no idea how disorienting it is to no longer be in danger every moment of every day. And to be myself 24-7, rather than some cover identity. I'm still getting my feet on the ground."

"Then you haven't decided what's next for you?" she blurted out and then snapped her jaw shut. If she could place her mouth literally under lock and key, she'd do it at this moment. Way to put the pressure on him right when he needed it least.

A grimace passed across his expression. "I've been conflicted about that. As I told you, I thought I knew what I wanted. Thinking about what life could hold next after the undercover assignment sometimes helped me stay sane. But something changed inside me during the time we were together. Then suddenly we were apart, and I needed to reorient my thinking and my values. It's been quite a chore. In the past week, you have no idea how many times I practically had to chop my hand off to keep from calling you to talk over my options, but I didn't want to put you under any obligation or expectation."

"Put *me* under obligation?" Trina gaped at him. "When I didn't hear from you, I figured maybe you wanted me in your rearview. You wanted to get on with your life."

Rogan's eyes widened. "I'm so sorry I let you feel that way, but how could you believe that after all we went through together? My problem hasn't been trying to move on from you, but how to stay."

"Stay?" The word emerged in a faint tremulous whisper. "What do you mean?"

"Let me explain."

"You'd better." Her heart throbbed in her chest. How could she allow herself to believe what she was hearing unless she understood what he'd been thinking?

"Here goes." He offered a faint smile beneath a gaze more tentative than she'd ever seen it. "I was only a little boy when my mom died and I started going on the road with my dad. Settled living was a thing of the past for the next decade. When I finally got into my first posting right after my DEA training and before undercover, it was in a major city, and I loved it. Yet now that I look back, what I loved was the work, not the urban environment. Actually, I got a lot of aggravation out of the traffic, and the pollution, and the press of people."

Trina reached out and grabbed his hand—not at all gently, the way he had held hers. "What are you trying to tell me?"

"Okay—" he grinned "—I'm getting to the point. I thought I wanted another big-city posting with lots of action and upward mobility in the agency, but being with you finally brought a truth to the forefront of my mind. The happiest I ever was in all my life was the three years I spent on my foster family's horse ranch. I looked forward to every new day—even if it meant mucking out stalls. I was never bored, and in those wide-open spaces, I felt the closest to God I've ever been. I'm as shocked as anyone to finally realize I'm not a city boy. I'm a country boy at heart."

A grin the size of Wyoming grew on Trina's face. "You've decided rural life might suit you?"

Hope was a stubborn flower to kill, so it had never quite left her, but now it burst into bloom.

Rogan answered her grin with a small one of his own. They weren't home free and together yet. He needed to find out something from her first.

"Yes," he said, "I like fresh air, open country, animals, sparse traffic and friendly people who enjoy living simply, but Trina, I still want to be a DEA field agent or maybe in some other kind of law enforcement down the road." He looked deeply into her eyes, gauging her reaction. "Probably why the upward mobility in the agency wouldn't be the best thing for me. Those higher pay grades are desk jobs. I'm not cut out for the safe work tucked away in an office."

Her smile had been fading as he talked, and his heart shriveled with the growing sobriety in her gaze. Here came the rejection when she told him again that she couldn't be with someone in a dangerous line of work.

"Rogan McNally," she said, "aren't we a pair? Both thinking we knew what we wanted, but both deceiving ourselves. I thought my torn-up heart needed to find a man in a low-risk profession—that I'd be safe then, too. Turns out being with you taught me differently. I'm wired to love a man of action."

"Love?" He blinked at her then grabbed both her hands and leaned in close to her face. "I already know I love *you*, but could you love a guy like *me* one day?"

"Not a guy *like* you," she said softly. "You!"

Rogan leaped from his chair, knocking it over. His whoop probably carried to the fellowship hall, but who cared?

Trina rose, laughing. "You see? A man of action."

Rogan wrapped his arms around her, lifted her from her feet and twirled with her.

"Ow, ow, ow," she protested, and Rogan set her down.

"I'm sorry. I forgot how bruised up you must still be. Forgive me."

"Of course. I enjoyed the dance, but let me heal a little bit more before you do that again."

"No worries. You are a lady of honor and integrity, and you deserve to be courted properly."

"Don't get carried away with the stuffiness." Her grin held mischief. "That's not either of us. You're a rough-and-tumble law enforcement agent, and I'm a country veterinarian with her arms elbow-deep in muck as often as not. But about this courting—how do you plan to do that? What sort of DEA posting can you get around here? I don't want you to leave a job you love. Of course, I could move my practice, as long as it's somewhere rural like you said. I—"

Rogan stopped her words with a finger against her lips. "Here's the best part of being the hero du jour. As I told you, I get to pick my posting. Just for me, they've designated an agent-at-large position to be based in Pinedale near where the action is—or where it will be once someone steps into the void left by Lawrence, Stathem and company and gets the illicit trade routes going again. Who better than me to spot what's going on?"

Trina let out a whoop that rivaled his own. "You're moving to Pinedale?"

"I haven't taken the job yet."

"What are you waiting for?"

"You to say you want me nearby."

"What do you think?"

"I think..." He moved in close and took her in his arms. "This."

Rogan lowered his head and tasted once more the lips of the woman he wanted to be with for the rest of his life. And as usual, she gave as good as she got.

EPILOGUE

One year later

Standing in the narthex of her church, Trina smoothed a bit of lace at the waist of her A-line satin gown and took Jim Miller's offered arm. The first strains of the wedding march touched her ears, and her heart began to pound fit to burst from her chest. In the next few seconds, she would walk through the double doors into the sanctuary, and Rogan would bc waiting for her with the minister up front.

This was Christmas Eve, *and* it was her wedding day! The first formal wedding with all the trimmings she'd ever had.

When she had married Rick, she'd worn a knee-length white sheath dress and he his military uniform for a quiet ceremony in a chapel near the base where hc was stationed, with only her dad and Rick's cousin present as witnesses. Nonetheless, it had been a beautiful occasion—a memory she would always treasure in her heart. Just as she was certain that Rick and her dad were still with her in her heart on this special day and that they would approve.

This ceremony was altogether different than that first one. Rogan and she had intended for it to be quiet and small, but as soon as the community found out about their engagement last July Fourth, that plan flew out the window. Everyone wanted in on the action. After all, Trina was the beloved area veterinarian, who went the extra mile—often literally—for her patients. And Rogan's popularity had developed from a hero protector to a dear friend as he participated enthusiastically in the things that mattered to the people in this rural area.

As a result, the church was packed with all their friends and neighbors, who went whole hog in contributing floral arrangements and her cascading bouquet of aromatic pine greens, berries and white roses, as well as all the homemade food for the banquet afterward. Who needed a caterer? A three-tiered wedding cake, courtesy of the Pinedale bakery, stood in a place of honor on a table in the fellowship hall. Of course, she and Rogan had already made a commensurate financial contribution to the county development fund. Everybody knew that. Nobody cared. Who was counting?

Today was for celebrating!

The double doors of the sanctuary opened, and smiling ushers in crisp dark gray tuxedos stood aside. One of them was a beaming, hale and healthy Jay Reynolds. The other was Ned Stinson, the agent who had led the rescue raid on Hadley's cabin. He and Rogan had grown to be good friends, and now after the first of the year, Ned was going to be joining Rogan in the Pinedale office as his partner. It turned out that there was a lot for DEA agents to do in this neck of the woods, and Rogan had already forged strong working relationships with local law enforcement, including the Shoshone Native police on the nearby Wind River Reservation. Of course, it hadn't hurt his credibility any that he was marrying a tribe member.

Jim patted Trina's hand, and she stepped forward with him. A concerted rustle traveled through the sanctuary as the congregation stood to its collective feet. All eyes riveted on her, but the only eyes that claimed her attention were the sky-blue pair at the end of the aisle. As she moved toward him, his eyes widened, and his lips spread in a welcoming smile.

Wow, he mouthed toward her, and tingles zipped from the top of her floral-tiaraed head to the tips of her satin slipper–clad toes. She canted her head slightly and returned the silent, appreciative *wow.* The very definition of handsome stood before her in a black tuxedo accented with a red vest. And he was all hers.

A grinning Jim handed her arm off to her husband-to-be, and the ceremony began. First the greeting, then prayers, then a brief, poignant homily on the gift of marriage, and then Trina handed her bouquet off to Amy Miller, her matron of honor, so she could take her groom's hands for the vows. Rogan and she had opted for the traditional and time-honored words of covenant—"till death do you part." Then a totally recovered Ethan Ridgeway—Rogan's best man—handed the rings to the minister, and they were able to say, "I thee wed," as they slipped the gold bands onto each other's fingers.

Rogan's hand was warm and ever so slightly trembly in hers. She met his adoring gaze as the minister spoke the words that sealed the union before God and witnesses.

"I now pronounce you husband and wife."

The minister was only beginning to add, "You may kiss the bride," when Rogan gathered her in his arms and did just that.

"Finally," he muttered against her lips.

"Forever," she murmured in return and wrapped her arms around his neck.

* * * * *

If you enjoyed this story, please look for these other books by Jill Elizabeth Nelson:

Lone Survivor
The Baby's Defender

Dear Reader:

I am so happy Trina and Rogan ended up together, as I hope you are also. They're such good people, and they deserve each other, especially after all the mayhem they faced and conquered as a team. Their story goes to show you can't tell how a relationship is going to turn out by the way it begins. Rogan and Trina's introduction to each other couldn't get much rougher than one holding a gun on the other. But after they got over that hump, they continually believed in one another and had one another's backs. That's the kind of relationship worth fighting for—the kind of relationship we want with special human beings and with the Lord.

It was my honor to tell this story in honor of the brave and dedicated men and women on the front lines of the war against drugs. I don't know about your family, but mine has been deeply impacted by the disease of drug addiction, a battle we continue to fight alongside our loved one. Thank God for breakthroughs that have happened and are to come.

I enjoy hearing from my readers and would love to hear from you at jnelson@jillelizabethnelson.com. You can find out more about me and my books at jillelizabethnelson.com. Looking forward to connecting with you through my future books.

Blessings,
Jill Elizabeth Nelson

WE HOPE YOU ENJOYED
THIS BOOK FROM

LOVE INSPIRED SUSPENSE
INSPIRATIONAL ROMANCE

Courage. Danger. Faith.

Find strength and determination in stories
of faith and love in the face of danger.

6 NEW BOOKS AVAILABLE EVERY MONTH!

LISHALO2020

COMING NEXT MONTH FROM
Love Inspired Suspense

Available December 1, 2020

TRUE BLUE K-9 UNIT: BROOKLYN CHRISTMAS
True Blue K-9 Unit: Brooklyn
by Laura Scott and Maggie K. Black

K-9 officers face danger and find love in these two new holiday novellas. An officer and his furry partner protect a police tech specialist from a stalker who will do anything to get to her, and a K-9 cop and a former army corporal must work together to take down a drug-smuggling ring.

DEADLY AMISH REUNION
Amish Country Justice • by Dana R. Lynn

Jennie Beiler's husband was supposed to be dead, so she's shocked when he rescues her from an attacker. Although Luke has no memories of his *Englisch* wife, now his Amish hometown is their only safe haven from a vengeful fugitive.

CHRISTMAS PROTECTION DETAIL
by Terri Reed

When a call from a friend in trouble leads Nick Delaney and Deputy Kaitlin Lanz to a car crash that killed a single mother, they become the baby's protectors. But can they figure out why someone is after the child...and make sure they all live to see Christmas?

ALASKAN CHRISTMAS TARGET
by Sharon Dunn

With her face splashed across the news after she saves a little boy's life, Natasha Hale's witness protection cover is blown. Now she must rely on Alaska State Trooper Landon Defries to stay one step ahead of a Mafia boss if she hopes to survive the holidays and receive a new identity.

CHRISTMAS UP IN FLAMES
by Lisa Harris

Back in Timber Falls to investigate a string of arsons, fire inspector Claire Holiday plans to do her job and leave...until her B&B is set on fire while she's sleeping. Can she team up with firefighter Reid O'Callaghan—her secret son's father—to catch the serial arsonist before her life goes up in flames?

ARCTIC CHRISTMAS AMBUSH
by Sherri Shackelford

After discovering her mentor has been murdered, Kara Riley becomes the killer's next target—and her best chance at survival is Alaska State Trooper Shane Taylor. Trapped by a snowstorm, can they find the culprit before he corners Kara?

LOOK FOR THESE AND OTHER LOVE INSPIRED BOOKS WHEREVER BOOKS ARE SOLD, INCLUDING MOST BOOKSTORES, SUPERMARKETS, DISCOUNT STORES AND DRUGSTORES.

LISCNM1120

SPECIAL EXCERPT FROM

LOVE INSPIRED SUSPENSE
INSPIRATIONAL ROMANCE

A deputy must protect a baby and her new temporary guardian.

Read on for a sneak preview of Christmas Protection Detail *by Terri Reed, available December 2020 from Love Inspired Suspense.*

"I'm going to find her." Nick Delaney shrugged off her hand. "She needs help."

"You're a civilian. Somebody trained to provide help needs to go," Deputy Kaitlin Lanz replied.

He flashed her one of his smiles, but it didn't dispel the anxiety in his eyes. "Then we can go together."

Digging his keys from his coat pocket, he held them out to her. "You can drive my Humvee. It's better equipped than yours."

"Fine." She plucked the keys from his hand.

"Come with me," Kaitlin said to Nick. Instead of immediately going out the door, Kaitlin stopped where the department's tactical gear was stored. She grabbed a duty belt and two flak vests. She tossed one to Nick. "Put that on."

Velcroing her vest in place, she grabbed her department-issue shearling jacket and put it on, covering her sweater. "Let's roll."

Once they were settled in the large SUV, Kaitlin fired up the engine and drove through town. Within moments, she turned onto the long winding road that led up the second-tallest mountain in the county. The bright headlights of the SUV cut through the darkness and bounced off the snow. They'd reached the summit near the gate of the estate when the SUV's headlights swung across the accident scene. A dark gray sedan with chains on the tires had slid off the road into a tree.

Nearby, a black SUV was parked at an angle and two men were dragging a female from the sedan's driver's seat. Kaitlin's hands gripped the steering wheel as she brought the vehicle to an abrupt halt.

Nick popped open his door and slid out.

"Wait!" Kaitlin yelled at him. The fine hairs at her nape quivered.

Were these men Good Samaritans? Or something far more sinister?

The men let go of the woman, letting her flop into the snow. Then both men swiveled to aim high-powered handguns at them.

"Take cover!" Kaitlin reached for the duty weapon at her side. She'd wanted Nick to appreciate her for the capable deputy she was, but not at the risk of his life.

Don't miss
Christmas Protection Detail *by Terri Reed,*
available wherever Love Inspired Suspense books and ebooks are sold.

LoveInspired.com

Copyright © 2020 by Terri Reed

LISEXP1120

Get 4 FREE REWARDS!

We'll send you 2 FREE Books
plus 2 FREE Mystery Gifts.

Love Inspired Suspense books showcase how courage and optimism unite in stories of faith and love in the face of danger.

YES! Please send me 2 FREE Love Inspired Suspense novels and my 2 FREE mystery gifts (gifts are worth about $10 retail). After receiving them, if I don't wish to receive any more books, I can return the shipping statement marked "cancel." If I don't cancel, I will receive 6 brand-new novels every month and be billed just $5.24 each for the regular-print edition or $5.99 each for the larger-print edition in the U.S., or $5.74 each for the regular-print edition or $6.24 each for the larger-print edition in Canada. That's a savings of at least 13% off the cover price. It's quite a bargain! Shipping and handling is just 50¢ per book in the U.S. and $1.25 per book in Canada.* I understand that accepting the 2 free books and gifts places me under no obligation to buy anything. I can always return a shipment and cancel at any time. The free books and gifts are mine to keep no matter what I decide.

Choose one: ☐ **Love Inspired Suspense Regular-Print** (153/353 IDN GNWN) ☐ **Love Inspired Suspense Larger-Print** (107/307 IDN GNWN)

Name (please print)

Address Apt. #

City State/Province Zip/Postal Code

Email: Please check this box ☐ if you would like to receive newsletters and promotional emails from Harlequin Enterprises ULC and its affiliates. You can unsubscribe anytime.

Mail to the **Reader Service:**
IN U.S.A.: P.O. Box 1341, Buffalo, NY 14240-8531
IN CANADA: P.O. Box 603, Fort Erie, Ontario L2A 5X3

Want to try 2 free books from another series? Call 1-800-873-8635 or visit www.ReaderService.com.

*Terms and prices subject to change without notice. Prices do not include sales taxes, which will be charged (if applicable) based on your state or country of residence. Canadian residents will be charged applicable taxes. Offer not valid in Quebec. This offer is limited to one order per household. Books received may not be as shown. Not valid for current subscribers to Love Inspired Suspense books. All orders subject to approval. Credit or debit balances in a customer's account(s) may be offset by any other outstanding balance owed by or to the customer. Please allow 4 to 6 weeks for delivery. Offer available while quantities last.

Your Privacy—Your information is being collected by Harlequin Enterprises ULC, operating as Reader Service. For a complete summary of the information we collect, how we use this information and to whom it is disclosed, please visit our privacy notice located at corporate.harlequin.com/privacy-notice. From time to time we may also exchange your personal information with reputable third parties. If you wish to opt out of this sharing of your personal information, please visit readerservice.com/consumerschoice or call 1-800-873-8635. **Notice to California Residents**—Under California law, you have specific rights to control and access your data. For more information on these rights and how to exercise them, visit corporate.harlequin.com/california-privacy.

LIS20R2

LOVE INSPIRED SUSPENSE

INSPIRATIONAL ROMANCE

IS LOOKING FOR NEW AUTHORS!

Do you have an idea for an inspirational romantic suspense book?

Do you enjoy writing faith-based suspenseful romances about courageous characters who are constantly threatened and must work together to overcome the danger?

We're looking for new authors for Love Inspired Suspense, and we want to see your exciting story!

Check out our writing guidelines and submit your Love Inspired Suspense full manuscript at
Harlequin.com/Submit

CONNECT WITH US AT:

www.LoveInspired.com

Facebook.com/LoveInspiredBooks

Twitter.com/LoveInspiredBks

Facebook.com/groups/HarlequinConnection

LISAUTHORSBPA0820R

LOVE INSPIRED

INSPIRATIONAL ROMANCE

UPLIFTING STORIES OF FAITH, FORGIVENESS AND HOPE.

Join our social communities to connect with other readers who share your love!

Sign up for the Love Inspired newsletter at **LoveInspired.com** to be the first to find out about upcoming titles, special promotions and exclusive content.

CONNECT WITH US AT:

Facebook.com/LoveInspiredBooks

Twitter.com/LoveInspiredBks

Facebook.com/groups/HarlequinConnection

LISOCIAL2020